A HOLMES FOR THE CZAR

From the Casebook of Miroslava Holmes

Gorg Huff & Paula Goodlett

Gorg Huff & Paula Goodlett
Visit my website at WarSpell.com

Printed in the United States of America

First Printing: Feb 2020
1632, Inc.

ebook ISBN-13 978-1-948818-70-4
Trade Paperback ISBN-13 978-1-948818-71-1

CONTENTS

In the years since the Ring of Fire, the influence of the up-timers was sometimes a mixed blessing. Depending on who you asked.

Both Bernie Zeppi and Cass Lowry were men in their twenties. Both had occasionally frequented strip clubs up-time before the Ring of Fire. Bernie, at the Gorchakov Dacha, got sucked into the history of strip clubs and found himself reading and translating articles on burlesque, Sally Rand and Gypsy Rose Lee, fan dancers, pole dancers and taxi dancers, which, Bernie learned, was where the 10 cents a dance came from.

Quick to see an opportunity, first bar owners and brothel keepers in Moscow, then in other cities in Russia, started incorporating this or that feature in their clubs.

By the time Cass Lowry arrived in Moscow in November of 1633, there were already such clubs in Moscow and Cass frequented and critiqued them. By the time Czar Mikhail left for Ufa, such clubs were common in many towns and cities in Russia.

PROLOG—KAROL & MARINA

Location: Moscow, Chernoff Estate
Date: June, 1636

K arol Karolivich Chernoff was hungover again. He rolled over in bed and groaned. Someone was ringing some god-awful bell somewhere.

"Master Karol, you have to get up. Your father wants to see you." The voice was his manservant's. The tone, as usual, wasn't as respectful as it ought to be, but still managed to sound nervous and fidgety.

Karol groaned again.

* * *

"It took you long enough." His father's voice also lacked anything like respect, but it at least lacked the nervous fidgety tones of the servants.

"Sorry, Father." Karol tried—and probably failed—to put respect into his voice. It was hard. He didn't feel any respect for his father. But the truth was Karol didn't respect much, not even himself.

"I have to go into the Kremlin. Mikhail has gone crazy."

"The czar?"

"Yes, the czar. Do you think I would care if one of your friends went crazy?"

Karol took a breath and didn't rise to the bait. "How has Czar Mikhail gone crazy, Father?"

"He's run off from the Dacha where Sheremetev was keeping him and freed all the serfs in Russia. He's trying to put us back into the Time of Troubles."

It took Karol most of the rest of the day to find out what was going on. His father was a supporter of the Sheremetev faction, and the corruption of his family disgusted Karol. That attitude was exacerbated by the Ring of Fire and the Gorchakov Dacha, not that he thought all that much of Bernie Zeppi or Cass Lowry.

Karol wasn't a great reader but he did read the pamphlets of the Flying Squirrel with interest and enjoyment. A true Russian philosopher. Not like the German want-to-bes at the Gorchakov Dacha.

Two days later, after seeing his father order one of the house slaves whipped half to death, Karol had had enough. He packed his bags, took his prize stallion and a spare horse, and left to follow Czar Mikhail to Ufa.

He caught a steamboat three days into his trip, and arrived in Ufa a week later.

Location: Ufa Docks
Date: July 15, 1636

Miroslava sat still on the deck of the river boat. The smells were wrong, the light was wrong, the sounds were wrong . . . everything was wrong, and she didn't want to be here.

"All right, girls, get a wiggle on," Madam Drozdov said loudly. Madam Drozdov did not shout. It was a matter of pride with her. Proper ladies didn't shout, therefore Madam Drozdov didn't shout. But sometimes she spoke quite loudly. Miroslava and the other girls who were owned in Nizhny Novgorod, but were contract employees here in Ufa, perforce "got a wiggle on."

It was one of Madam Drozdov's favorite phrases, one she'd learned from Cass Lowry. She liked it because it applied to the girls in her employ in two ways, aside from meaning get to work as it did in the up-time. It also referred to the fact that the girls major employment was to wiggle. Wiggle bottoms, wiggle breasts, wiggle in general.

Miroslava thought it was over-used from the second time she'd heard it. But Miroslava, by now, knew to keep her opinion of such things to herself.

She got in line behind Marina, another of the girls. Like Miroslava, Marina was now a contract employee rather than a slave.

But Marina was normal. Not crazy like Miroslava.

Miroslava's eyes flicked along the dock, seeing the wood planks and the tree posts driven into the river bed to support the planks. She saw the ripples of the river as the water circled around the posts. Miroslava saw everything. She always had. And she remembered everything she saw, heard, smelled, tasted, or felt.

And the smells, sights, sounds here were not the smells, sights, and sounds of Nizhny Novgorod.

They were *wrong*.

"How much bribe?" Marina asked Miroslava. She indicated the approaching city guard, or maybe port official, with her chin.

Miroslava tried to calculate. Number of girls, amount of goods, condition of the port . . . she didn't have enough information. There were too many holes in the thing in her head that figured out such things. She could see the numbers and made up symbols before her eyes, but too many spots were too blank for her to solve.

"I don't know," she said.

Marina grinned. Marina got a kick out of stumping Miroslava.

* * *

As it happened, the bribe was lower than either girl would have guessed. It was also more complicated. Ufa had been a fort and a fur trapper's outpost before the czar arrived, so the city government was familiar with bars and brothels. And what Madam Drozdov wanted to set up was close enough to those two things that it was well within Olga Petrovichna's scope. Olga was the wife of the official outpost commander of Ufa before the czar arrived a few days ago. But she'd been running things for years, and, with the support of Anya, she still was.

The largest issue was the status of the girls, considering Czar Mikhail's proclamation of emancipation, but Madam Drozdov was prepared for that. She had signed contracts of debt and employment for each girl. Those contracts certified they weren't slaves or serfs. They were contracted employees. Which was enough to keep the czar off her back, which was all Olga really cared about.

So, in exchange for a reasonable bribe, Madam Drozdov got permission to put up her club. She still had to buy the land.

She rented, and had refurbished, a building already built. The contracts also gave Madam Drozdov control over—but not ownership—of the "land" the czar promised escaping serfs. The land wasn't necessarily in the form of actual territory. It could be converted, sold to the Bank of Russia in Ufa, for cash. So Madam Drozdov had a healthy bank account to have the repairs made, and the girls got a couple of weeks off as the building was being refurbished.

Location: Ufa Docks
Date: July 18, 1636

Karol watched as his horses were led off the steam-powered river boat. The steamboat wasn't one of the ones made by the Gorchakov Dacha or the Gorchakov factory in Murom. It was one of the ones converted by the boat's owner from the instructional broadsheets, and Karol was mostly just happy to have survived the trip. He looked around. There was a hill and on top of it was a curtain wall made of trimmed tree trunks. Karol grabbed a dock worker by the arm. "Is that the Kremlin?"

"Yeah, sure," the man said, and pointed. "Just follow that street around."

Karol tied the lead of his spare horse to Socks' saddle and mounted for a short ride.

As he rode, he looked around. Ufa was a city of tents. The Kremlin was there and built, but outside it, what had been only weeks ago a small fur trapping outpost was now filled with tents set in orderly rows. The river boats that ran with the czar weren't the only ones, and even they were traveling back and forth, picking up people and goods to bring here.

* * *

Two hours later, Karol found himself in a medium sized room with a window that was just a hole in the wall with shutters. The czar and czarina were seated in wooden chairs on a little platform and Bernie Zeppi was standing in a corner along with some guards.

Karol bowed, wondering why he was here. It wasn't like he was a regular at court back in Moscow.

Czar Mikhail waved him to stand. "We're glad to see you, Karol."

"Your Majesty?"

The czar smiled. No, he was grinning. "You are the highest ranking Chernoff to come to our colors so far. Congratulations. You are now the owner of all the Chernoff lands in Holy Mother Russia. That may change if another of your relatives decides to join us, but at this point it seems unlikely."

"I don't want it!" Karol blurted. Then, feeling the need to explain, he said, "Your Majesty, I came here to serve you. To serve Russia. Not for personal gain."

The czar was looking at him like he was a . . . a . . . something. Possibly a saint. More likely a madman. Then his expression calmed as though he'd decided which. "I understand and appreciate the nobility of your motives, but it will actually help us if you accept your family's lands. It's one of those up-timer things. We're limited in the amount of money we can use by the property we have to back it. But we can use your property back home, though, according to my chief banker, at a considerable discount. Never mind. Even if you don't use it, if you accept it, it will be in the bank and the bank can make loans based on it."

"Then of course I accept it, Your Majesty. But I won't touch it."

"That's entirely up to you," the czar said. "And since you're not going to use it, what are you planning on doing?"

"Whatever Your Majesty commands."

That led to about fifteen minutes of questioning. The truth was Karol wasn't qualified to do much. He'd spent his life hunting and gambling, and avoiding work of any sort. He could ride a horse, shoot a bow or a rifle, play cards and dice, he was competent—but not really good—with a sword, and he was literate. But that was about all.

Because of his rank—and the fact that he was one of the very first high ranking nobles to arrive here—he was put in charge of the city garrison, and instructed to listen to his sergeant.

✳ ✳ ✳

The Ufa city garrison wasn't a full time military unit. It was made up of craftsmen, mostly *streltzi*, who spent most of their time in other jobs. Many of them, especially those like him who arrived by river boat, brought their shops with them. Not the building, but all the equipment. Butchers brought their cutting tools, shoe makers their lasts, tailors their sewing machines, and so on. Some also brought their bows or guns, but priority was given to the stuff they would need to practice their craft.

Location: Garrison Room, Kremlin
Date: July 19, 1636

Yuriy Kotermak looked up as the young man came into his cubbyhole. Yuriy could read and write, but not very well, so he did all he could by memory. But some reading and writing was unavoidable. He stood. "Good morning, sir," he said to the teenaged boy who was his new commander.

"Sit, sit, Sergeant," Karol Chernoff said, "and tell me what I'm supposed to do. I want to get to know the men."

Yuriy didn't roll his eyes. Apparently, his new captain was a liberal. There were worse things, Yuriy supposed, but he couldn't think of any right now. The function of officers was to stay out of the way while the sergeants ran the companies, and the last thing he needed was this boy trying to chat up his men while drill was going on. He had few enough men, and most of what he did have were odds and sods from all over. Anyone who was able to get a seat on a river boat.

Then Yuriy had a thought. There was a new club setting up only a couple of blocks from the Kremlin, and a lot of the younger men would be going to the opening. "Well, sir, chatting with the men during drill is not a good idea. But off duty, you could go to the opening of the Happy Bottom Club. A lot of the younger lads will be there."

Location: The Happy Bottom, Ufa
Date: July 28, 1636

Opening day at The Happy Bottom was boisterous, exciting, and so far mostly disappointing. Madam Drozdov, the owner of the new club, came from Nizhny Novgorod, brought her cadre of bar girls with her, and hired a river boat for the trip. The building was still very much in the process of refurbishment.

Karol was here because his *streltzi* were here. Not that Karol was new to such places, but the ones he frequented generally charged more and were fancier.

Then he saw her.

Marina was a vision. Strawberry blond hair and green eyes, with a bright friendly smile that seemed to be just for him.

He bought her drinks. He bought her meals. And he bought private dances.

He bought so much over the next couple of days that his absolute refusal to touch his drawing account that represented his family's ill-gotten gains crumbled in the face of his need for cash.

Having broken into the funds, he used them. He rented a suite in the nicest hotel in Ufa, still under construction. And then went to see about getting Marina free of her contract.

Location: The Happy Bottom, Ufa
Date: August 2, 1636

"I want to buy Marina's contract."

Madam Drozdov nodded sagely, and named a figure that was only mildly outlandish.

For a moment Karol was ready to argue.

Then he thought about his father's face when he got the bill, and he paid with a smile.

✳ ✳ ✳

Marina liked Karol well enough. He was a cute boy. He had long brown hair and a blonde beard, recently trimmed to copy the style adopted by Czar Mikhail. Mostly, though, he was young and strong, with fairly even features.

She pulled his head down to her and kissed him. It wasn't bad, but he could use a bit of instruction. So she showed him some things by example, and he caught on fairly quickly.

It was hours later that they blew out the lamps and went to sleep.

Location: Karol's Rooms
Date: August 3, 1636

Marina woke to the sunlight shining into her room. Karol was still snoring gently beside her. She pushed his shoulder. "Hey, sleepyhead. Don't you have drill today?"

He pulled the pillow over his head and mumbled, "They don't need me. The sergeants can handle it."

"Of course they need you. You're a very important man, and it's an honor for them to have you in command."

She could tell that he didn't believe her, but that he wanted to. So she laid it on thick. Eventually, she got him ready and off to the day's practice.

* * *

Karol's command wasn't made up of full-time soldiers. His command was *streltzi* who had other jobs five days a week. On one day a week, a squad at a time, they drilled under the sergeant while Karol stood around and watched. It was marching in a row, and using pikes, because most of them didn't have guns. Not even matchlocks, much less the new chamber-loading flintlocks, or the even newer chamber-loading cap locks.

He spent the day watching them march, and went home to find a bored and quite put-out Marina. Her day was spent in the rooms without any money to buy breakfast or lunch. Karol had eaten with the squad that practiced today.

* * *

At dinner, in an inn a block away from the rooms, Marina listened to his discussion of the lack of proper equipment that his squad possessed. "Well, you're their commander. You buy them boots and guns. And while you're at it, you can buy me some things too."

The truth was that Marina was more interested in the things that he could buy her, but she was smart enough to know that it would go over better if she also encouraged him to buy gear for his soldiers, whether he did or not.

Karol was entranced by the notion. Here, finally, was something noble he could do with his family's money. Something that would help the troops under his command.

Location: Drill Field
Date: August 4, 1636

"Sergeant." Karol waved and Yuriy, grimacing slightly, came over. "I have some banking matters to take care of. I'm minded to buy boots and rifles for the men, but to do that I am going to need to arrange for the funds."

"Thank you, sir." Yuriy sounded, for the first time, like he really meant it. "Do you mind if I ask what brought this on?"

"It was Marina's idea."

"Well, sir, please thank her for thinking of us."

✳ ✳ ✳

The Ufa branch of the Bank of Russia was located, for now, in the Kremlin. It was manned by three of the Dacha crew who were specializing in economics. They were mid-level dvoriane and their bank was, for right now, just a spare room in the Kremlin with three small tables and stacks of papers held together with twine.

But it worked. Karol arranged for a checkbook for Marina and learned that new guns couldn't be had for love or money in Ufa. There were several bootmakers among the *streltzi* in the city. There might even be some in his company, and Karol remembered that there were. From the bank, he went back to the rooms to see Marina.

"What's this?" Marina asked when he handed her the checkbook.

"It's a checkbook." He opened it and showed her the checks. They were a standard print, but these had a number stamped in the upper left hand corner. "They are going to print a proper one for you, but that will take a couple of weeks. These will do until that's ready. What you do is write the amount in this box, and sign your name in this box . . ."

She put a finger to his lips. "Karol, I can't write. I can't even sign my name, much less write out number words."

"Oh, sorry. I didn't think of that. Ahh?"

"How about you just give me an allowance in cash?"

"I can do that."

After a short detour to the bank to pick up some banknotes and some copper kopek coins, they proceeded to the bootmaker's shop.

And so it went for the next few months. His nights were bliss, and his days were busy with discussions of what the men needed, partly with his sergeant, and later as the garrison grew, with his sergeants, and partly with Marina.

Location: Karol's Rooms
Date: September 3, 1636

Their room was new. The building was new. It was owned by the same man, but as the new building was finished, the man had moved them in. It was rough boards, daubed smooth and whitewashed, with stands for lamps and shuttered windows that the innkeeper insisted would be getting glass windows soon.

Marina woke up and moved to the chamber pot in a rush. She bent over and emptied her stomach into the pot. Karol was asleep. She looked over at his sleeping form and was terrified. Terrified that he would think it wasn't his, because by now she was sure that she was going to have a baby. She knew Karol well enough to think that he would see to the baby's support if it was his. And she thought it was his.

Depending on just when it was conceived.

So she worried as she took the chamber pot down the hall to the washroom and emptied it into the larger container. That container would be taken away by a wagon on Friday, and replaced with an empty. The contents were sold to the tanners and the chem shop at the Dacha. She rinsed out the pot and took it back to their rooms, wondering how she was going to tell Karol.

* * *

The truth was Karol wasn't sure that the baby was his, but at this point he was so enamored of Marina that he didn't much care. It was hers, and that was good enough. So he reassured her, told her he believed her about him being the father, and promised to see to its welfare. He even considered marrying her. Considered it, but didn't act on the thought.

The baby was having an effect on Karol's thinking. He was the head of the Chernoff family, at least here in Ufa. And, as unlikely as it sometimes seemed, if Czar Mikhail were to win the war, he would be the head of the Chernoff family entire.

He knew the rules. He couldn't marry Marina, not if his family were to maintain its status. But he could have an acknowledged bastard, and give that child a place in the family.

Location: Karol's Rooms, Ufa
Date: December 3, 1636

Then one night about five months after he bought Marina's contract, he put his hand on her belly and the little fellow kicked. He laughed. Timing or not, this was his baby. His son.

Karol laughed with joy. He went to the window and opened the shutters. The window, as promised, had glass now. Sort of small diamonds of translucent greenish glass held together with lead came. He looked out at the stars and knew in his heart that he had a son. The city of Ufa was different now. Most of the tents were now buildings, and new tents were put up farther away from the Kremlin and the New Dacha with its own walls.

It was a new world.

The right world for his son.

The very next day he went to the Kremlin and officially registered the child as his. He also sent a telegraph message off to his father, telling him he was going to be a grandfather in a few months. Partly, it was due to true attachment for the child and Marina, but there was also the very real desire to stick out his tongue at the stuffed shirt who was so very conscious of his birth and rank, but never let that noble birth slow him when going after a profit that more properly belonged to someone else.

He told Marina that he was going to acknowledge the child when it was born, and that night Marina rewarded him in the best way she knew how. He didn't try to explain that the papers were already in place at the Ufa Kremlin.

Location: Moscow, Chernoff Estate
Date: December 12, 1636

Karol Ivanovich Chernoff listened as his clerk read the insulting telegraph message, and fumed. The news of Mikhail's destruction of the dirigible, *Czar Alexi*, was all over Moscow, along with the story about the children's argument and Evdokia's settlement.

It was a poke in the eye of the Council of Boyars and the Sheremetev faction. It also suggested that things weren't going well. There was a real chance that Mikhail might win.

It still wasn't the way to bet. At least, Karol wasn't prepared to change the family's bet. But it was starting to look like a real possibility.

And now this. The telegraph was sent in clear text, so every telegraph operator from Moscow to Ufa knew that the Chernoff family was about to have the child of a whore added to its ranks, and that his idiot younger son was going to acknowledge the little bastard.

His first response was to send a telegraph of his own, disinheriting his son. The problem with that solution was that he'd already done it. Every single great house who had a family member in Mikhail's camp, of necessity, disinherited that family member as soon as it became known that they were with Mikhail.

The assumption, unstated, was that if Mikhail won, or if he lost, there would be a rapprochement between the family and the disinherited. But, in the case of his idiot son, Karol wasn't at all sure how the family would come out, especially if there was a bastard son to put ahead of his older brother or cousins.

He considered openly putting a price on the heads of the child and the whore mother. But he couldn't do that. For if Mikhail won, Karol Karolivich would refuse any rapprochement. In his whole life, Karol Ivanovich had never met anyone as stubborn as his second son.

He even considered having Karol Karolivich murdered, but that would leave them with no foot at all in Mikhail's camp.

It took Karol Ivanovich two days to figure out what to do. Then he called in a scribe and sent for a Cossack known to the family.

Location: Moscow, Chernoff Mansion
Date: January 4, 1637

Ivan Grigoriyevich Shkuro had light brown hair and a short beard. He was a skilled soldier, and not afraid to get his hands dirty. He went where the money was and didn't concern himself with questions of right and wrong. If there was a god, he was going to hell. He'd known that since he'd killed his first man at thirteen, over ten years ago now. At this point, it was grab all the joy out of life he could and that took money. He looked around the back hall in the Chernoff mansion, wondering what he could get away with stealing.

His unfortunate conclusion from the way the servant eyed him was "nothing." *Oh well, it was just a passing thought.* He followed the servant into Karol Ivanovich Chernoff's study.

He bowed, but not that deeply. He was a Cossack, and Cossacks didn't bow.

Karol Ivanovich Chernoff snorted. "Still the same stubborn fool, I see, Ivan."

"I am what life has made me, Colonel Chernoff."

"It's not the world. You were born an evil bastard."

Ivan shrugged. Maybe it was true, but if it was, what did that say about the people who hired him, save that they were too gutless to shoot their own dogs?

Karol Ivanovich Chernoff tilted his head at Ivan. "I need you to kill a woman. Do you have any problem with that? I could find someone else."

"I don't have a problem with it."

"Good. She's a whore in Ufa."

"Any particular whore?" This might actually be fun.

"Yes, a very particular whore. Marina is her name."

"That's not enough. I don't know how many whores there are in Ufa—"

"The one that's taken up with my idiot son. I want you to shoot her in the belly and let her bleed out. That will solve all the family's problems."

"So I go to Ufa and ask your son?" Ivan's lips twitched in a smile.

"No. You can't let Karol know about it."

"You're talking about a lot of work and a lot of risk, Colonel. I will have to travel all the way to Ufa in winter, avoiding armies, track down your son, then find his woman, who may well be protected, and kill her without him finding out that you're involved."

Karol Ivanovich named a sum, and they started bargaining. Ivan, of course, refused to take paper money, insisting on silver coins. He got mostly English and Polish coinage, but there were a few of the USE silver coins in the mix.

It was quite a bit of money, and he had the promise of the same again, once it was done.

Ivan set off the next day.

Location: Karol's Rooms, Ufa
Date: February 14, 1637

Marina was definitely showing now, and Karol smiled as he came in the door carrying takeout. "Hello, Dominika. I have food." He held up the paper bag. There were paper plants outside several Russian cities and quite a lot of it made its way to Ufa. Less now, with Kazan besieged, but still some. The waxed paper bags were worth a quarter kopek when returned to the restaurant.

Karol carried the bag to the table, and started pulling out the wooden tubs. There was a shop with a power lathe right here in Ufa that made them, but they were also returnable for a deposit. Dominika would, he knew, be given the sack and the containers and would collect the deposit. She was Marina's friend, and he liked that it helped her.

"How was drill?" Marina asked.

Karol, much to his relief, was no longer the commander of the Ufa garrison. He was now a company commander, the commander of Company A. Colonel Timofei Fedorovich Buturlin was the new commander and Karol was just as happy about it. He didn't feel qualified to command a battalion.

"We got the new chambers for the AKs, and spent the day dry firing and cleaning. Tomorrow, we'll be practicing against targets. How was your day?"

"I spent more of your money," Marina said with a smile. "There is a bakery down the way, and they needed new fire bricks to expand their ovens. In exchange, you have a ten percent interest in the bakery. I don't think it will pay you back anytime soon, but it's what you said you wanted. Only investments that 'help the people.' "

He leaned over and kissed her.

"Let's eat," Dominika said.

Location: Karol's Rooms, Ufa
Date: April 5, 1637, Two Hours
Before Dawn

Marina was as big as a house, and terrified. Everything was going so well before the Kazakhs came. And now Karol, the stupid fool, was running off to get himself killed before he legitimized her baby.

"It will be fine, my love. General Izmailov is a great general, much better than General Tim. He knows what he's doing. We'll go out and give the Kazakhs a drubbing, and be home for dinner."

Marina wanted to believe him. She wanted desperately to believe him. But while Karol was strong and handsome and brave, he wasn't quite as bright as he might be, so Marina couldn't bring herself to trust his judgment in military matters.

Besides, even if General Izmailov won the day, that didn't mean Karol would be safe.

He kissed her, a sweet and gentle kiss, then stood and ran from the room.

Marina fretted. She couldn't just lie here. She got up and started to get dressed. Then the contractions started. They came fast and hard.

No! They couldn't be real. They were early. She had a month to go.

But they were real.

Fifteen minutes later, after several more contractions, her water broke.

Marina screamed for aid, and the manager called a midwife.

Five hours later, at the very moment Karol was leading his company out to face the Kazakhs, Larisa was placed next to her mother's breast for her first meal.

* * *

Karol led Company A out into the field. They were carrying AK 4.7s that he'd bought them, wearing good boots and heavy leather buff coats that had some chance of stopping an arrow, though would do little against a rifle bullet.

Karol was proud and utterly terrified. And as much as anything else, the thing that kept him marching was the knowledge that less than a mile behind him, his love and his unborn child were defenseless if he failed.

"Cock! Aim! Fire!" Karol shouted and swung his sword down, as the gunsmoke cleared enough for his men to see. The results of the previous volleys weren't nearly as good as he'd hoped. They were, he thought, doing some damage, but not enough. And his boys were getting scared. A few started to run, and Karol threatened to cut off the balls of the next man who ran. "Our wives and lovers are back there, men, and we're all that is standing between them and those bastards! Stand your ground!"

An arrow hit his buff coat, and the thick leather coat slowed—but didn't stop—it. What would have been a killing blow simply cracked a rib. But it was on his right side, so when he raised his sword again, his whole right side screamed in agony. But—by will—he forced the arm up and with tears streaming from his eyes waited for the gunsmoke to clear. "Cock! Aim! Fire!"

The sword came down and almost slipped from weakened fingers, but he held it, seeing Marina's face in the smoke. He had to keep her safe. The rest of the army was running, but his battalion was standing firm.

Well . . . partly.

Stefan's company, Company B, was solid, but his people were starting to slip away. "Close up on Company B, Yuriy. Don't let them panic."

He saw Yuriy knock a man to the ground with the butt of his AK, and for the life of him, he couldn't remember the man's name. Just that he was a tailor with a brother in the company and a wife in Ufa. Then an arrow hit Yuriy, and he went down.

Karol pushed men to the right, closing his company up to Company B. The arrows stopped, and Karol looked out, hoping the Kazakhs had had enough.

No such luck. Karol knew horses. They were readying a charge. "Get ready, men," he shouted. "They're coming!" He tried to lift his sword, but it wouldn't come up. He tried harder, and got it shoulder high.

Then there was no more time. The Kazakhs were charging. He stooped below the lance and swung his sword at the horse's legs. He hit, but the blow knocked the sword from his weakened grasp.

The horse fell and rolled over him.

Another stomped on his belly as it ran over him.

He saw Marina's face.

Then nothing.

Location: Outside Ufa
Date: April 4, 1637

Ivan Grigoriyevich Shkuro sat his horse well away from the battle, and realized that he wasn't getting into Ufa. Not without greater risk than he was willing to take, and not with his horse. Ivan was fond of the horse. He'd bought it in Moscow right after he took this assignment. He'd ridden it from Moscow to Nizhny Novgorod, and from Nizhny Novgorod to Kruglaya Mountain, from Kruglaya Mountain to Kazan, where he'd had to go the long way around to avoid the army investing the place. Then, finally, to here. Just in time to be blocked by the thrice-damned Kazak Khanate investing Ufa.

This was getting ridiculous.

He looked over at the horse. "You may be bad luck, Star. Ever since I've had you, it's been one army in my way after another."

The horse tried to nibble his hair.

CHAPTER 1—A FIGHT AT THE HAPPY BOTTOM

Location: The Happy Bottom, Ufa, Russia
Date: April 15, 1637

T he lights were the new Coleman lanterns, inside and out, and young boys earned coins running around and pumping up the lanterns as needed. There were dozens of people waiting to be admitted, most of them armed and dressed as soldiers including the western Russian army armbands, as well as the outfits of Cossacks and the soldiers of the Kazakh Khanate. It was a soldier's club with lots of booze and other drugs, much of which was shipped up the Ufa River from the Volga, in spite of the war. The winter trade continued with only occasional interruptions. As much came in winter as in summer, because the ice made a perfect road once it was deep enough.

The club had a big sign over the wide double doors proclaiming "Girls! Girls! Girls!"

The line advanced. Feliks stepped through the door, and was allowed into the even better lit foyer. To the right as he entered was a cloakroom with a counter, and an attractive, scantily clad woman backed by a large armed man.

"Check your weapons and coat."

It wasn't a question. You couldn't get into the club proper with weapons, but they were very good about keeping them safe until you came back with the tag. He passed over his sniper rifle and his pistol, even his bandolier of loaded chambers. Also his great coat. In return, he got a wooden token with a hole in the top and a number painted on it. The number matched a tall box built into the walls of the cloakroom, tall enough to hang a coat or store a long gun or both. There were no doors on the boxes, just the tags, and people watching the stuff.

This stop was most of the reason for the line of people out into the cold.

Pocketing his token, Feliks went through a single door into a large, much less well-lit room. There were some bright spots.

There was a stage at the far end of the room. At the moment, it was occupied by a bunch of women dancing to an amplified record player. The stage was lit by more Coleman lanterns. These had part of the chimney mirrored, turning them into flood lights, lighting up the dancers.

The space behind the bar was well lit for the making of drinks and the counting of money.

Feliks headed for his table, looking around for Fiana. She was dressed in a short skirt and one of the new "corsets" that were popular in Moscow. They weren't, Fiana told him, real corsets, just cloth with brass and tin spangles. Hers was red. A really bright red from one of the dyes that the Dacha produced. She was in white makeup, with ruby red lips. She had a tray of vodka, put a mug on a table, got paid, and gave the soldier a kiss on the cheek. Feliks didn't like her having to work here, and he didn't like it when she kissed other men. But, in spite of his rank—he was a sergeant—he couldn't afford to buy her out of her contract.

So he glared at the man and went to his chair, which wasn't occupied at the moment, and ordered a vodka.

He paid Fiana, and got his own kiss, then drank the pale green liquid in two gulps and ordered another.

* * *

Two hours later Feliks was slurring his words a bit, and begging Fiana to marry him every time she brought him a drink. A big man came in. He had a still fresh scar on the right side of his face from a bullet that had come within an inch of killing him.

Feliks knew who he was. He was Egor Petrovich, who worked in Stefan Andreevich's gun shop, and was with him at the battle in the field. Egor was a part-time soldier, but he had money because he worked in Stefan's gun shop and the lucky bastard got let go without having to pay a ransom like he should have.

Feliks didn't like Egor. He especially didn't like the way he was always grabbing Fiana.

"Bring me a beer, Fiana," Egor bellowed. "A big one." Then he sat in the chair, almost breaking it. Egor was big, which was another reason that the five foot three Feliks didn't like him much.

Fiana waved her free hand, and yelled, "Coming right up."

Less than a minute later, she was at Egor's table, bending over to put the large stein of beer onto the small table. Egor, the bastard, put one arm around her hips and pulled her close. With the other arm, he pulled three of the red and gold bills from his pocket and put them down into her corset. Fiana wiggled and pushed her breasts against his hands and kissed him on the lips.

The first Egor knew about it was when Fiana was pulled away from him. She fell backwards over another customer, pulled by a hand around her arm. Then Egor felt the fist hit his cheek, slide off it to break his nose, and at that point Egor knew what to do.

He jumped up and grabbed the little bastard who'd hit him and squeezed while the little man pounded on his back. The little bastard was stronger than he looked, and when he changed targets to the sides of Egor's head, Egor shifted his grip and threw the little bastard.

That knocked over more tables in the crowded club.

Shortly afterward, the bouncers interrupted, and both Feliks and Egor were ejected from the side door of the club.

Egor walked around the corner to the front of the building and went in just far enough to retrieve his coat and pistol, then went home cursing the name of Feliks Pavlovich.

✳ ✳ ✳

Ivan Grigoriyevich Shkuro climbed from the floor after the big man threw the little bastard onto his table. His tunic was covered in the local vodka and beer, and one arm had landed in some sort of dipping sauce. He clapped with the rest as both combatants were thrown from the club, then asked

Marina who they were and what it was all about. He smiled at her as she explained. She would be dead soon.

The explanation somewhat exonerated the big man in Ivan's view, but that little shit who was so proud of the sniper patch on his tunic. . . . He needed some sort of punishment. Even after Ivan finally got into the city, finding Marina turned out to be more work than he would have expected. Karol Karolivich was dead, making him hard to track. And by the time Ivan got through with that, the girl was gone from his house. The landlord neither knew or cared where, but did inform him that she'd had her brat on his good sheets on the very day of Karol's death.

A bribe to a clerk got the news that Karol had legitimized the little bastard while still in the womb. So Ivan was planning to kill the girl just as instructed, then tell the clan about the babe. He was in this soldier's club because he'd finally gotten the story of Karol and Marina from one of the sergeants in Karol's company, along with the word that Marina was back in The Happy Bottom serving drinks now that Karol was dead.

It was Marina who brought him his beers, the one before the fight and the one after it.

He finished his new beer and went to the exit. He asked the guard, "What do you know about that little shit who started the fight?"

The guard shook his head in disgust. "That's Feliks. There's his rifle, right over there."

Suddenly Ivan was struck with an idea. There was his crossbow, just three of the little cubicles down from the rifle. Why not trade his crossbow for the rifle? He showed his shirt sleeve to the guard and made the suggestion.

"I can't do it. Tomorrow Feliks will show up, and if his gun is missing, there will be hell to pay."

Ivan was disappointed, partly because he was planning to use the rifle to kill Marina later tonight. But then he had another thought.

"All right, I understand." He scratched his beard. "How about this? You don't give me a thing. Just switch my stuff for Feliks', like we got the wrong tickets or something. No real harm done, but it will inconvenience the bastard. And I don't need my crossbow for a while. There's a ruble in it for you."

Not seeing any harm in it, the guard agreed, and the deed was done. What the guard didn't realize was that Ivan was a thorough man. He knew the shifts at The Happy Bottom, and he knew that this guard would be going off shift at midnight. And there would be three hours after that for Ivan to pick up the rifle before the club closed.

He would shoot Marina with Feliks' gun.

35

Two hours later, Ivan strolled in the front door, handed over his ticket and collected Feliks' gear. All of it.

CHAPTER 2—MURDER IN THE NIGHT

Location: An alley in Ufa
Date: 3:30 AM April 16, 1637

Ivan stood in the alley and waited, watching the side door of the Happy Bottom. The door was thirty-seven of Ivan's paces away. He had carefully paced off the distance yesterday. He was also beginning to think that the rifle was a bad idea. The iron barrel wasn't just heavy. It was long. Holding the cursed gun level was worse than holding a pike steady. At least with the pike, the pike butt was on the ground and if a pike blade moved an inch or two, who cared.

The side door opened. He lifted the gun to his shoulder, and took careful aim. Ivan was a strong man. He braced himself against the building and waited, looking down the sights. The girls were milling about in the light of a Coleman lamp held on a stick.

There!

His target was talking to another girl. He took a breath and held it. The other girl moved, and he squeezed the trigger.

The rifle slammed against his shoulder like the kick of a mule.

When he looked back at the scene, the wrong girl was down.

Everyone was running around and a few moments later, well before he had the chamber out of the rifle, Marina was back in the club and it was not looking like she was going to come out again anytime soon.

* * *

Two hours later, in his room, he looked at the rifle and quietly cursed himself. He never should have let his resentment of the asshole in the bar make him change his plans. The local cops were going to be looking for a rifle. If one was missing from the Happy Bottom's cloakroom, it wouldn't be long before they knew just who took it. That stupid guard would talk his head off.

Ivan didn't just kill people. He also stole stuff. He'd picked locks before, even the new locks. This, however, would be a first.

The first time in his life that he'd broken into someplace to put something back.

It wasn't one of the new locks. A string and some wires did the job. His gear was in Feliks' box, so he took his, and returned Feliks', not even keeping a few rubles for himself.

To the devil with it. I'll use my crossbow.

Location: The Happy Bottom, Ufa, Russia
Date: 3:30 AM April 16, 1637

Anatoly opened the side door and lifted the Coleman lantern on the rod, then stepped out into the alley. He looked around for cut purses, muggers, and horny bastards, then waved out the ladies. It was part of his job, after all. They came out, colored cloaks over their regular clothing, faces washed of the makeup they wore at work. They milled around, talking to one another. Or complaining to one another, as their individual personalities dictated.

As they were starting to separate to go to their homes, Anatoly heard a shot.

Fiana heard the shot too. Then the bullet hit her. It went between two ribs on the way in, ripped the carotid artery to shreds two inches above her heart, then bounced off the right scapula and exited out her right side. Eight feet later, going much slower, it buried itself in a heavy wooden wall.

People were screaming and Fiana didn't know why. She was coming out of shock and the pain was just starting. She turned and the lack of blood to her brain made her stumble and fall. She fell onto the wet, cold ground and the light of Anatoly's Coleman lamp was the last thing she saw.

* * *

Marina screamed and ran. She didn't see where the bullet came from, but she ran anyway. There were no more shots.

* * *

Miroslava didn't run. To outward appearances, she was frozen in shock. That wasn't the case, not exactly. The truth was she was trying to figure out what had happened. The shot came from somewhere, but where?

Miroslava's brain didn't work right. She knew that. Her mother had told her. Her father had told her. The priests had told her. Everyone told her. When something weird happened, she had to stop and figure out what was going on. It could take from a few seconds to minutes, but she was pretty much useless until she figured it out. It was a dangerous way to live, and the truth was that if Miroslava weren't so pretty, she would probably be dead by now.

In this case, the bullet couldn't have been shot by someone close. First, the shot wasn't loud enough. Second, there was the time between the sound and the bullet hitting Fiana. Like lightning, but backwards. The sound arrived before the bullet. Then there was the fact that no one was armed. Certainly not with a rifle. And there was no smell of gunsmoke in the air, like there would be if it was fired from nearby. This was a rifle shot at night.

About then Anatoly grabbed her arm and tried to push her back into the Happy Bottom.

"Put out the light, Anatoly. You're letting him see us."

"What? Get inside where it's safe."

It was over an hour later that Miroslava was finally allowed to go home. They were asked if anyone saw the shooting. Miroslava hadn't. She wasn't looking in the direction of Fiana or the shooter, who was probably standing next to a building across the alley and a block away. She was looking at Marina. She knew where everyone was, but they didn't ask that, so she went home.

Home was a rooming house. Twenty small rooms, each just large enough for a cot, and with only a curtain between them and the hallway. But there was a place where you could put a locked trunk to hold your goods, and the old man who owned the place would notice if anyone tried to take a trunk out.

Location: Barracks, Ufa, Russia
Date: April 16, 1637

Feliks Pavlovich woke with his head banging, and Tadeas Tadeavich shaking his foot. He kicked air and groaned.

"Where's your rifle, Feliks?"

"What!" Feliks looked around and didn't see his rifle. Also missing were his pistol and his great coat. It took a little while. Feliks wasn't feeling well. Then he had it. He got thrown out of the Happy Bottom last night. His rifle was still in the checkroom of the bar.

"What's the time?" he asked.

"Eight, I think. Maybe a bit after."

"Shit!" Quickly as he could, given his condition, Feliks put on his boots. He was still wearing his pants and underclothes from last night.

"Tell the master sergeant I'm in the crapper. I'll be back." Then he ran.

It only took him five minutes to get to the bar. It was located fairly close to the Ufa Kremlin. When he got there, the place was quiet. He banged on the front door.

* * *

Marina was just getting back to sleep after feeding the baby. She wasn't up to dancing yet, so she got stuck with all the unpleasant jobs. It was how she paid for her and the baby to stay here. "What do you want?" she yelled through the door, trying both to be heard by the banger and not wake Madam Drozdov or the baby.

"I need my rifle and my great coat!" Feliks said.

Marina recognized the voice and the face through the eyehole. She let him in, took his claim check, then gave him his rifle, pistol, bandolier, and great coat from the shelf. Neither of them noticed that one of the chambers of the bandolier was empty.

Marina closed the door and went back to her cot. Between Fiana being shot and the baby crying, she'd gotten maybe two hours sleep last night and was so tired she wasn't tracking. By the time she got back to her cot, she'd forgotten who it was that knocked. And by the time she woke up that afternoon, she'd forgotten that there had been anyone.

Gorg Huff & Paula Goodlett

CHAPTER 3—WHO CARES?

Location: Factory of Stefan Andreevich, Ufa
Date: April 19, 1637

Egor Petrovich knocked on Stefan's office door, and Stefan assumed it had to do with the drop forges. That was Egor's job, after all. This was Stefan's first day back at work, and he was still very much on light duty after the battle, which was why he was stuck in the office with his arm taped and his ribs wrapped.

"What's gone wrong now?" he asked, the pain making his voice rougher than he would have preferred.

"Nothing with the forges. This is something else."

Seeing the expression on Egor's face, Stefan used his good arm to awkwardly wave him in. "What's wrong?"

"Fiana's dead and the cops aren't even looking for the murderer."

"Who's Fiana?"

"She's . . . She was . . . a bar girl at the Happy Bottom," Egor said.

And Stefan knew why the streltzi cop force wasn't looking very hard for the killer. They didn't much care, and they surely didn't want to offend some *Deti Boyar* or *dvoriane* by accusing him of the murder of a bar girl. "Cop" was one of the new words introduced by the up-timers. Before then the city guards were less concerned with fighting crime than manning the walls in case of attack. That was still partly true, but nowadays most good-size towns—which Ufa was becoming—had cop forces that patrolled the streets and offered some protection from robbery and assault.

What Stefan didn't know was what Egor thought Stefan could do about it. It took Stefan that long to remember that he was now Captain Stefan Andreevich Ruzukov, a member of the service nobility in his own right. It was a recent occurrence and there was a lot going on. The constitution of New Russia was only days old and Ufa was still being rebuilt after the attack by the Kazakh khanate. They were back in the main building, but not yet back in production. It turned out that the Kazakh army hadn't burned down their building.

That still left the question. "What do you want me to do about it? Egor, I don't know how to find a murderer."

"I know who did it," Egor said. "It was that bastard Feliks."

That required a bit of explaining. Apparently Fiana had Egor, Feliks, and perhaps several others on her string, and Feliks was the jealous type. Egor was willing enough to share and realized that Fiana had probably liked his money more than she liked him. But he cared for the girl and her death hit him pretty hard.

Egor was with Stefan in the battle, and he'd stood his ground with the rest of them. That was a bond that couldn't be ignored.

"So, if I push an investigation, it might come back on you?"

"I'd never kill Fiana, sir. And besides, I wouldn't shoot someone from a block away."

"I'm not accusing you, Egor. I'm just pointing out that this Feliks character isn't the only one with a motive. I doubt I could get the cops to investigate on just my say so."

"What about the Honorable?" Egor asked.

That was a good question. Stefan's wife, Vera Sergeevna, was a delegate to the Constitutional Convention, and now that they had a constitution—even if it was so far only ratified by the Kazakh khanate and the cities of Kazan and Ufa—she was likely to become one of the first representatives in the new Congress of Eastern Rus.

Vera probably could get an investigation started. Not that Stefan was sure that was a good idea, but she was the one to talk to.

* * *

That night in their townhouse—they lived in Ufa now, not New Ruzuka—Stefan asked Vera what she thought.

"I don't know, Stefan," Vera said. "I remember how you almost got executed for murder."

"Well, to be fair, I did kill the man. It was an accident and in self-defense, but I did kill him. Apparently this young woman was shot from a distance. That could hardly be self-defense."

"That's not my point," Vera said. "I just don't have a lot of faith in the deductive powers of the cop force—That's it!"

"What's it? What's what, for that matter?"

"Vasilii Lyapunov, is it. He's an engineer who worked on the steamboat engine design, and he loves up-timer mystery stories. He was in the congress, which is how I know him. Now he's back at work in the new Dacha here in Ufa, and swears he will never involve himself in politics again."

The New Dacha, or Ufa Dacha, wasn't actually a dacha, which meant the private farm or country house of a Russian noble. The New Dacha was the rebuilt Dacha in Ufa where, even now, they were working on rebuilding the technological base from the Gorchakov Dacha outside of Moscow.

"Why would Vasilii Lyapunov be interested?" As it happened Stefan knew Vasilii. He was a nice enough man, in the sort-of-distracted way that was fairly common among the scholars of the Ufa Dacha.

"Because he loves mysteries. Everything from Sherlock Holmes to the *Murder She Wrote* and *Quincy, M.E.* books."

"What?" Stefan had not the slightest idea what she was talking about. He could read and write his own name, he could even—slowly and with effort—make his way through a report on the cost of iron or the effect of replacing the gear on a drop forge crank. He had never read a word of the Bible. That's what priests were for. And in his entire life, he had never read a single word for entertainment.

"He likes to read for the fun of it," Vera explained. "There are books in the new Dacha that have stories in them, and some of those stories are stories about mysteries, even murder mysteries."

"Why would anyone want to read something like that?"

Vera shrugged. "You like listening to ghost stories on a long winter night. I know you do."

"Good enough. You think he would be interested in this situation?"

"I can ask. I'll go over to the Dacha tomorrow and do that."

Location: New Dacha, Ufa
Date: April 20, 1637

The Dacha was a walled compound next to the Ufa Kremlin. It was a combination research center and university, even though the university part was just getting started.

It took Vera a few minutes to find Vasilii. He was giving a lecture on steam engines. With a model on a wooden bench, he showed how it worked. Vera sat in the back of the room while he was talking, and while he answered a series of questions. Some seemed to Vera to be good questions. Others seemed to be silly.

* * *

As the class was breaking up, Vera walked down to the lectern, where Vasilii was explaining something to a young man.

Then he turned to her. "What can I do for you, Vera? Are you and Stefan going to start building your own steam engines?"

"No. This has to do with your other interest."

"Politics? That's not an interest. That's a curse. I'm out of it, and never going back."

Vasilii was a member of the liberal wing of the Dacha group. He was disgusted by the compromises on the issue of slavery and serfdom they ended up making. "Not that either," Vera said. "I'm here about a murder mystery."

"What? You want to borrow my books?"

"No, Vasilii. You know I only read Russian, not up-timer English. Now, if you will let me finish before explaining that it can't be, or asking questions, you might find out why I'm here."

Vasilii held up his hands, "I yield to the Honorable Delegate from New Ruzuka."

"There was a murder at the Happy Bottom on the night of the fifteenth. One of the bar girls was shot, and no one has been arrested or charged. I haven't talked to the cops, but from what I have been told they aren't investigating it. I was wondering if you would like to pretend to be . . . Dr. Watson, is it? Or Mr. Marple."

"Miss Marple. Vera, why do you care?"

"Because, Vasilii, one of our employees, Egor Petrovich, cares,. Egor was with my husband on the field."

"Very well. I will look into the matter. I'm not a real detective, but there aren't any real detectives, are there?"

"Not here at any rate," Vera agreed.

Location: Ufa Kremlin
Date: April 20, 1637

Colonel Evgeny Ivanovich Aslonav looked up. He recognized the clothes more than the man. "What can I do for you, sir?"

"Vasilii Lyapunov, Colonel. I'm from the Dacha and I am curious about a recent murder."

That was a surprise. What did this fellow care about peasants killing peasants in street fights and drunken brawls? "Which one? We've had three in the last week."

"A young woman, Fiana Ivanovna, a bar girl. Shot outside the . . ."

Vasilii trailed off at Evgeny's wave.

"I know the one you're talking about. Not much to it. No one knows who did it and no one much cares, either."

"Well, a friend asked me to look into it. So, what can you tell me about it?"

"Not much, but wait a moment." Evgeny got up from the table he was working at and went to the door. "Kazimir, go find Pavel Borisovich and have him come to my office."

He turned back to the Dacha man. "Pavel was the one called to the scene. He can tell you more."

Pavel, it turned out, was a short, somewhat paunchy man in a faded green-dyed broadcloth tunic with two black stripes on a yellow armband indicating the rank of corporal in the city guard. He also wore a thick leather belt with a truncheon in a holster. His hair and beard were brown, starting to go gray. "Happy to help, sir."

They left the Kremlin and Pavel asked, "Why are you interested, sir?"

"I read murder mysteries, so a friend asked me to investigate."

"Murder mysteries? Careful of the puddle there, sir."

Vasilii avoided the puddle and explained about murder mystery books.

Pavel didn't say anything. But the way Pavel didn't say anything got Vasilii's attention. Russia was still a very class-driven society, and while *streltzi* were above peasants, they were well below a well-placed *Deti Boyar* like Vasilii. Especially here in Ufa. Working at the Dacha was high status. "Speak freely, Pavel. What do you think?"

"Honestly, sir, it strikes me as a bit silly," Pavel said, still hesitant. "Most murders are simple things. Two men fighting over something, usually a woman or money. One wins, the other dies, and we hang the winner." He didn't add "unless the winner is a noble."

"Sometimes it's a man and a woman fighting, and then it's usually the woman who dies. And we hang the man." Again the unspoken proviso "unless the man is a noble."

"So, who are you going to hang for this one?" Vasilii asked with a grin.

Pavel shook his head. "This is the other kind. They're less common, but they do happen. This is the body in the street murder. No one knows who did it or why." Pavel took a breath. "Even with these we mostly know why because we find their purse gone. That tells us someone killed them for their money, but there are a lot of people killed for their money. And we mostly don't know who did the killing."

"But Fiana's purse wasn't gone, was it?"

"No, and that's the most surprising thing about this case. Even if the killer wasn't after her money, I would have thought one of the other whores would have taken it."

"Not the fact that she was shot from a distance?"

"We only have the witness' word for that," Pavel said.

"You think they are all lying?"

"Maybe. Some because they have something to hide. Some because they are afraid of their pimp or the club owner."

They were walking as they talked, and they came to the Ufa mortuary, a new addition since the Czar's arrival and over full at the moment. Most of the common soldiers who died in the battle were buried with some ceremony in what was coming to be known as Soldiers Field. But some officers, mostly, were actually being embalmed and getting head stones.

Meanwhile, the everyday people of Ufa—however they died—were piling up. Ufa had plenty of ice since winter was just ending, so there were a lot of chilled bodies in the basement of the mortuary.

* * *

The mortuary attendant appeared to share Pavel's view that this was a fool's errand. But he showed them to the body, then stood by as they examined it. They found the entry wound and the exit wound, which meant Vasilii's hopes were dashed. "I was hoping the bullet would still be in her."

"Whatever for?" asked the morgue attendant.

"Because you can tell which gun the bullet came from if you have the bullet."

"How?"

So Vasilii explained about the grooves cut into the bullet by the rifling and how it is unique to each rifle, like a fingerprint. That, in turn, led to an explanation of fingerprints, complete with Vasilii showing his finger tips and comparing them to Pavel's and the morgue attendant's.

The morgue attendant was a serf from Nizhny Novgorod, who followed General Tim up the river because he didn't want to be a serf anymore. This was what he could find in the way of a job and he was okay with it. Dead bodies didn't bother him.

Vasilii told him about *Quincy M.E.*, explaining what a medical examiner was a doctor that examined dead bodies to determine how they died.

"I don't know about cutting into them. It seems sort of disrespectful. What if they feel it?"

"They don't," Vasilii said.

"How do you know?"

Vasilii looked at the man. He was taller than Pavel and thin, younger too, and for a moment Vasilii was considering suggesting that he study to become a medical examiner. But the man probably could barely spell his own name. He would look for one of the doctors that Tami Simmons trained. Tami was the up-time nurse who came to Russia to be Mikhail's family physician. Mikhail appointed her Surgeon General for Russia shortly after they arrived in Ufa. As Tami put it, it wasn't that she was qualified, it was just that there was no one else in Russia who wasn't even less qualified.

In this case, though, the cause of death was fairly apparent, so a full autopsy was probably not necessary. Still, Vasilii thought Ufa needed a medical examiner.

"Thank you for your help," He said to the morgue attendant. "What's your name by the way?"

"Waldemar, sir."

They took their leave, and Pavel suggested they get lunch.

"That's a good idea. Let's go to the Dacha cafeteria."

The Dacha cafeteria was a part of the Dacha and was manned by cooks from the Dacha back outside of Moscow. It was one of the best places to eat in Ufa because it used equipment brought from the original Gorchakov Dacha. Franklin stoves and woks, frying pans and rotisserie grills.

It was also exclusive. The workers at the Dacha and their guests, and that was it. Well, the czar and czarina sometimes ate there.

Location: Dacha Cafeteria
Date: April 20, 1637

The room had south-facing windows. The glass had a greenish tint, and came in small sections about four inches across, held together by thick lead came. At this time of day the windows filled the room with light and warmth. There were wood tables and checkered tablecloths, and you got your food by going through a line and picking it up. There were wood trays to carry it back to the table. It was all very fancy to Pavel's eye, but Vasilii was used to it from his time at the original Gorchakov Dacha.

He got to the end of the line where a woman was seated with a box and a hole puncher. Vasilii pulled out his meal card, and pointed at Pavel. "He's with me."

Karina punched two holes in the lunch column of Vasilii's card and handed it back.

"Karina, do you know where Tami is?" Karina started life as a slave on the Gorchakov estates. She was now a free woman and knew everyone in the Dacha.

"She should be here in a little bit. She has a class on infectious diseases that should be ending about now."

"Would you ask her to drop by my table when she comes in?"

"Sure."

* * *

They were eating stroganoff and cheese with mushrooms and little sausages, good black bread, and peas on the side when Tami Simmons arrived.

"Karina said you wanted to see me?" Tami said, holding a tray with one hand.

"Have a seat. If you have time, I would like to talk to you about getting a medical examiner for Ufa."

Tami nodded, and took a seat. "That's not going to be as easy as you might think. Both the Russian Orthodox church and the Muslims hereabout have issues with desecrating the dead. It's made doing any sort of work on corpses politically challenging."

"I hadn't thought of that," Vasilii admitted. He scratched his short-trimmed beard. "We may be able to help each other if the city government of Ufa could be persuaded to install a medical examiner. That might let us find the bodies for your classes."

"I'll talk to Olga Petrovichna and see if we can get anything arranged." Ufa had fairly unique status in New Russia, Eastern Russia, the Real Russia, whatever you want to call it. It was the capital and it was a state in the federal system. What that meant was still being worked out. The Constitution was still only confirmed by Ufa, Kazan and the Kazakh Khanate. No legislator was yet seated, or elected, for that matter. The laws, such as they were, were temporary decrees issued by Czar Mikhail, or by people like Olga's husband, Stanislav Ivanovich Polzin, officially appointed as mayor of Ufa. Like the nation, the city of Ufa was still trying to figure out how to elect a government.

They talked about the legal status and duties of a medical examiner, and what to propose. In spite of Vasilii's oath that he would never again be sucked into politics, his time as a delegate to the constitutional convention left him with considerable knowledge of how politics worked. If they could get Olga to agree, she would convince her husband and the czarina, and that would make it happen.

Pavel watched all this with something like shock on his face. These were, if not the movers and shakers of New Russia, at least people who knew them to talk to.

"See, Pavel? You're going to have a report to make to your commander," Vasilii said.

Pavel swallowed.

Location: Alley Next to The Happy Bottom

After lunch, Vasilii and Pavel went to the scene of the crime. Vasilii had Pavel describe where the girl's body was found, and while he was drawing the outline of the body in chalk, one of the girls who worked in the bar came up the alley and knocked on the door to be let in. That brought the bouncer, Anatoly, to the door, and that brought several of the other girls that worked at the bar.

Pavel started to tell them to get back inside and mind their own business, but Vasilii wanted to question them, so they were told to wait.

Vasilii went to the wall and started looking for the bullet.

"What are you doing?" a female voice asked.

"Looking for the bullet."

"You're looking in the wrong place," the girl said.

"And how would you know that?" Pavel asked the girl, who shrank back and said nothing.

"It's all right, Pavel." Vasilii waved the cop back, and looked at the girl. She was a bit on the tall side—he guessed five foot seven—and thin, but still with enough curves that it was quite clear she was a woman. She had auburn hair, and since she wasn't yet wearing her makeup, he could see that she had freckles. Not a lot, just a few on her cheekbones, which were high on a heart-shaped face. The early afternoon sunlight turned her eyes bright green. "Now, Miss, what's your name?"

"Miroslava," said the girl. She was wearing a fur robe and there wasn't much on beneath it. She was one of the girls who came out to see what was going on, and Vasilii assumed that she was getting dressed for work when they showed up.

"Very well, Miroslava. What makes you think I'm looking in the wrong place?"

"Because you are," Miroslava answered. Then, as Pavel started forward, she added, "She turned when she fell."

"You were here at the time of the murder?"

"Yes."

"Where were you standing?"

She pointed and he had her stand on the spot and face the way she was facing that night.

"And that's the way you were facing when the shot was fired?" Vasilii asked.

"Yes."

"But if you were looking in that direction, you couldn't have seen her when she was shot."

She didn't say anything, but Vasilii could tell from her expression that she was not convinced by his logic. Now his curiosity was aroused, so he asked, "How do you know which way Fiana was facing?"

"Because she was calling Marina a whore, and Marina was standing there. And because if she was standing the way you thought, the person shooting would have had to be in that wall there, and there was no one there."

Vasilii looked at the wall where she was pointing. It was clearly in her line of sight. He visualized the scene. Where Miroslava was standing she could see Anatoly, the club's bouncer, the missing Marina, and the wall where the shooter would have to be if the bullet entered Fiana's body from that angle. She had to have turned when she fell. The girl Miroslava was right.

"Very good," he told her.

She rolled her eyes again. In the different light they were a rich, warm brown.

"So which way was Fiana facing when she was shot?"

Miroslava pointed.

Vasilii followed her pointing finger to the wall of the club, then walked over to where Fiana was standing on the night of the murder and faced the point Miroslava indicated.

He shook his head. "No, Miroslava. It still doesn't work."

She turned to face him, then said, "You're facing the wrong way."

"I'm facing the way you said she was facing."

"No, you're not."

"Yes, he is," put in Pavel, and several of the girls who were watching the re-creation murmured agreement.

Miroslava's face turned red, and one of the girls said, "That's done it. Miroslava's going into one of her moods."

Vasilii looked at Miroslava, then at the girl, and was even more curious. He stepped back and said, "Miroslava, please show me how she was facing when the shot was fired."

Begrudgingly, Miroslava walked over and took a position facing the wall of the club with one hand up, pointing at someone who wasn't there.

Pavel started to say something, but Vasilii held up a hand. There was something about the way she was standing and the way she was facing. Then he had it. Miroslava was facing the way Miroslava said Fiana was facing the night of the murder. Not at the same point, but in the same direction.

Vasilii had faced the point Miroslava pointed at, but Miroslava was standing in a different place when she pointed, and he'd asked for direction, not target.

Vasilii didn't think he had ever in his life met someone as literal minded as Miroslava.

"Do you see it? She is facing the same direction she said. Not the same point, in the same direction."

Pavel just looked confused.

"Never mind, Pavel. She wasn't lying. She's just more precise than most people."

Vasilii went back to his calculations. Remembering his books and the lines that stretched from point to point described in the books, he drew a line in his mind that went through the space where Miroslava stood, then followed that line to the wall. He walked over about fifteen feet and started examining the wall about four feet above the ground. He wasn't finding anything.

"What are you doing?" Miroslava asked.

"I'm looking for the bullet." He turned back to her and the concern or perhaps confusion on her face.

* * *

Miroslava looked at him, and something was wrong. She looked at the ground where Fiana's body fell the other night.

She walked back to where she was standing when Fiana was shot, then retraced her steps as she'd gone to see the body on the ground. She saw in her memory the bullet holes, the small entry wound and the slightly larger exit wound.

And now she knew what was wrong. The wound where the bullet came out wasn't just bigger. It was longer, not round. The bullet didn't come out facing the same way it went in. By now everyone knew what bullets looked like. They weren't balls like the old guns shot. They were little short spears like a crossbow bolt without the feathers. And this one was facing down when it came out of Fiana.

It didn't go straight through Fiana's body. It must have hit something and bounced, so when it came out of her it was going in a different direction. "You're still looking in the wrong place."

"Where should I be looking?"

She pointed to a place about six feet to his left and almost at the base of the wall.

* * *

Vasilii looked at her, followed her pointing finger, shrugged and moved to where she directed. And sure enough there was a white spot where the bullet knocked a piece of the bark of the log loose. The Happy Bottom was a log building. That was common in Ufa—and Moscow, for that matter. Using a knife, he cut some of the wood away, then tried to pull the bullet out with his fingers. It didn't budge. "I'm going to need some tools, Pavel. You wait here while I go back to the Dacha and get them."

"That's fine. I'll hold our murderer while you're gone."

"What?" Vasilii looked up to see Pavel holding Miroslava's arm.

"She couldn't have seen the bullet hit if she was where she said she was," Pavel explained. "So if she didn't do it, she knows who did."

Miroslava was looking angry and terrified.

"Don't be silly, Pavel. You've already seen that Miroslava can tell things that other people can't."

Pavel didn't release the arm. He just looked stubborn. "It's a trick, a cheat. Next thing she'll be claiming Fiana's ghost told her where the bullet went."

Vasilii stood up. "Look, Corporal. I know you would like this to be over, but you have no motive. You have no murder weapon. All you actually have is the fact that Miroslava is more observant than most. There is no reason to believe she is the murderer, and very good reason to believe that she can't have been."

"And what would that be, sir?" Pavel was starting to sound positively belligerent.

"The bullet. I can't be sure of much about it until I get it out of the wall, but I can already see it's a copper-jacketed bullet."

Copper jackets were not common in pistols. They weren't even common in normal rifles. They were hunting and sniper rounds, because the copper coating held the round together better and kept the barrel cleaner, both of which made them more accurate at longer ranges. But they cost twice as much as a regular lead round.

"It's a reasonable supposition given what you knew, Pavel, but she didn't do it. Fiana was shot with a rifle from a distance."

Pavel looked around the alley. It was around fifteen feet wide and the buildings on either side of it were short on windows. Pavel looked up at the top of the buildings, but they were slanted to slough off snow. No good place to stand, and the angle didn't work either. "From where?"

Miroslava pointed. "There. Two blocks down, across the alley. At first I thought it was a block away, but that doesn't work."

Pavel shook her. "How do you know that?"

Miroslava looked at him and her face went red again. So did her upper chest, which was exposed by the robe opening.

"Let her go, Pavel," Vasilii said. "She's Sherlock Holmes, that's all."

"What?"

"Her mind works differently. She isn't the murderer, but she can help us with the investigation."

"She has to work," said Anatoly. The big man was just standing there watching, until then. "She has a contract and she owes the owner fifteen rubles."

"Fifteen rubles!" Vasilii blurted. "You have to be joking." Looking at Anatoly, Vasilii perceived that he wasn't joking at all. "I want to see that contract and your books."

"Not my books," Anatoly said. "Madam Drozdov owns the club."

"Fine. I will want to see the contract and her books. And so will Olga Petrovichna."

It took a while to get it worked out. One of the girls was sent to the Dacha with a note to Vadim, a *streltzi* craftsman who worked with Vasilii on steam engines and other projects. Vadim had no interest at all in murder mysteries, but he was fond of pretty girls.

Meanwhile, Vasilii took possession of Miroslava from Pavel and took her inside so he could have a chat with Madam Drozdov. It turned out that Madam Drozdov was acquainted with Olga, and the contract was legal as far as it went. And the books were in order, even if the prices that the girls were charged for makeup, rent on their dressing room, and—as best

Vasilii could tell—the air they breathed while in the club, were exorbitant. To put it mildly.

Vasilii was not an ivory tower intellectual. He knew how the world worked, which was the reason that he was one of the people that the Dacha chose to be a delegate at the constitutional convention. He was fully aware that he couldn't save the world. But Miroslava was special. He wanted to think that it was the uniqueness of her mind that enthralled him, but the truth was that her beauty was a part of the reason for his interest.

Not being able to think of what else to do, he paid her debt and bought her contract. It was a general employment contract, light on the specifics of her duties, and Vasilii had no idea what he was going to do next.

* * *

Next, it turned out, was Vadim and the tools from the Dacha. The bullet was carefully removed from the wall and examined. He showed Pavel and Miroslava the striations on the bullet and assured them that they were unique to the gun, and that a comparison to other bullets would let them tell the difference.

"And that would help if we had a bullet to compare this one with," said Pavel.

They had spent most of the day on this, and Vasilii had other work to do and so did Pavel. Grudgingly, Pavel released Miroslava into Vasilii's custody with warnings not to run off.

* * *

Miroslava examined Vasilii Lyapunov. He was dressed in good clothing, and there was ink on his right forefinger and thumb, and a spot in his left cuff, so he wrote. Both hands had contact with the paper for some reason. His shoes were the new left and right in the new combat boot style that was becoming popular in Ufa. His pants were the up-time jeans, black. Black—really black, not the dark gray that was more common. Black was expensive dye. A much more expensive dye than woad.

He was wealthy, well-educated, not bad looking, though his teeth were a bit crooked and he had a bump on his nose. His hairline was receding, but not badly yet. And he was fidgeting like he didn't know what to do. He wasn't a pimp. "Should we go to your rooms now?"

"What? Yes, I guess so, until we find some place for you to live."

"I have a room," Miroslava said. Not all the girls did. She didn't like the idea of taking anyone to her room, but he owned her contract. So if he wanted to go, he could go.

Miroslava always kept her agreements. It was all she could do to keep the world sane. She was worried about how she was going to pay the rent at the rooming house now.

"Let's go there, then. I will see you home and we'll figure out what to do next. You are in my custody so it might be better if you stay with me," Vasilii said as though he was just now working that out. He owned her contract, and she was under suspicion in the murder and in his custody, so she would have to stay with him until she was cleared.

"It's this way." She walked, leading him, and being careful of where she put her feet. Four blocks away, they got to the small building that held her room. It was seven feet wide and eleven feet long.

"This isn't a room. It's a closet," Vasilii said.

The room had a cot, two and a half feet wide, and five feet long. It rested on her two trunks. The trunks held her collections. Miroslava didn't know how to explain her collections. No one understood them, not even her. They were rocks and animal hairs, and things that made no sense to anyone but her. But, in her mind, they fit together and having them and ordering them made her feel better. Made her feel calm.

Vasilii looked at the room. It wasn't actually a closet. That was just a phrase that he learned from a book. It was very small. Too small for a person to live in. But also it was very, very clean. The wood floor was smooth and flat, as though someone had used a stone on it to polish the wood. And, in a corner, was the stone. The daub walls were whitewashed, and the small lantern was covered so that the smoke would collect on the chimney, and not reach the walls to discolor them. There was a rag, neatly folded, over the stone. Probably to be used to wipe down the walls. There was a heavy blanket on the cot, so that she could survive cold winter nights without the sort of stove that Vasilii had in his rooms at the Ufa Dacha. It wasn't a pleasant place to Vasilii's way of thinking, but work had been done here. A lot of work to make the place as clean and orderly as possible.

Vasilii looked at it and thought of his own rooms. He had three. His workroom, his bedchamber, and his sitting room. There was also the cafeteria, where he ate most of the time, but that wasn't his room. And there was the jakes down the hall. The Ufa Dacha was the first place in Ufa to get indoor plumbing, even before Czar Mikhail's residence, and the bath house. There wasn't actually much construction at the Ufa Dacha. As soon as they got something working, it moved to one of the factories in town.

But Vasilii's rooms were a mess most of the time. Not dirty, but Vasilii tended to leave stuff where it was when he finished with it. Twice a week a maid came in and cleaned the place, putting things away. The rest of the time things were wherever Vasilii had last put them down. He wasn't all that sure Miroslava would appreciate the change. But he wasn't leaving Miroslava in this place. He just couldn't.

During the battle with Salquam-Jangir Khan's forces, the Ufa Dacha became emergency quarters for the more well off of the citizenry of Ufa, but those people were moving back out into the open space now, some of them living in double-walled tents.

Vasilii talked to the old man who owned the flop house, and informed him that Miroslava would be moving. He also hired two men to carry Miroslava's trunks and other possessions to the Dacha.

* * *

The rooms in the Dacha were large by Miroslava's standards, and the toilet was a revelation. She was curious as to how it worked, and flushed it three times, examining the way the float worked to control the flow of water into the tank. The cafeteria was another revelation, and aside from the fact that Vasilii was a slob—not unusual among men—it was a very nice place.

She saw his drafting board in his workroom and realized where the ink on his sleeve came from. She looked at the drawings of things she didn't know enough to understand, and wanted to understand.

Vasilii said, "Let's go to see Anya and get you a bed." Anya, who was now married to Filip Petrovich Tupikov, was the manager of the Dacha. She wasn't part of the scientific staff. Instead, she was the top boss of all the support staff. She was the person that would arrange for a bed to be brought to Vasilii's rooms and also for Miroslava's meal ticket, the paper card with squares to be punched out as meals were eaten in the cafeteria. Anya was also the person in charge of the Dacha commissary, which for convenience sake was where Vasilii bought grooming supplies, ink, paper, and pens. He assumed that Miroslava would need grooming supplies too, and more.

Location: Ufa Dacha
Date April 20, 1637, 4:30 PM

Anya was up to her ears, as Bernie would say. Peace with the Khanate was only declared eight days ago, and though the damage to the outlying town proved much less than they feared since the Khan's forces hadn't gotten around to burning the outer city, it was still pretty extensive. As well, Ufa was constantly in a state of overcrowding, so she had people stacked on top of each other.

Anya didn't have a computer, not even an aqualator, though there were some of those in the Ufa Dacha. She had a typewriter, a mechanical calculator, and three secretaries.

Vasilii Lyapunov was the only member of his family in Czar Mikhail's Russia. They were a Gorchakov connection and were quite well off, but most of the family was less than enamored with Vladimir and Natasha and decided to stay home. They were probably all dead now, all but Vasilii. So if Czar Mikhail won, Vasilii Lyapunov would end up owning some fifteen villages and a small town. He was also quite a good mechanical engineer and was doing good work on the design of new steam engines and boilers. About half the steam engines in Ufa were designed by him. So were the steam engines used in the dirigibles. At the moment, he was working on what he called an airplane steam engine system. Not for a single engine plane, but for a larger plane. Specifically, Vasilii bought the plans for the Jupiter 4 and intended to put the boiler in the body, the condenser in the plenum, and the motors in the wings.

The main reason that Lyapunov had been spared a roommate was the money. Anya was one to keep her eye on the ball, and Vasilii's credit account in the Russian National Bank, Ufa Branch, was huge.

It was also the reason he was allowed past her secretaries to see her in person. Vasilii came in, followed by a very pretty auburn haired woman a bit taller than average, but not much, even features, but the giveaway was the clothing. The cheap finery that tried to imitate the dress of a noblewoman, but failed to carry it off. Anya remembered being dressed that way.

"What can I do for you, Vasilii?"

"I'm going to need an extra bed for my rooms and a meal card for Miroslava." He pointed at the girl.

"Why do you need another bed?" the girl, presumably Miroslava, asked.

"For you to sleep on," Vasilii said, a blush crawling up his cheeks.

Miroslava was looking confused, and Anya—who had seen the world from both Miroslava's and Vasilii's positions—assumed that she wasn't all that bright. She was certainly pretty enough, a lithe figure, wavy auburn hair under a *povyazka*, the traditional headgear of unmarried women.

"He's trying to look noble," Anya said. Then, looking at Vasilii's blush, added, "Maybe he's actually being noble."

Miroslava looked at Anya and back at Vasilii and said, "He bought my contract. The one bed is fine."

"You bought her contract." Anya lifted an eyebrow. Vasilii was a bright shade of pink now.

"Ah . . . She's a material witness in a murder investigation."

"And that required that you buy her contract?" Anya asked, playing with him, then seeing how embarrassed he was, decided to let him at least a little off the hook. "It's none of my business."

"No, no! It's— She's a female Sherlock Holmes."

Oddly enough, Anya did know who Sherlock Holmes was. Bernie Zeppi had mentioned him and his sidekick Doctor Watson several times, and she was aware of Vasilii's obsession with murder mystery stories. As it happened, Anya preferred science fiction. At least when she had the time to read for pleasure, which wasn't often. She looked at the woman again. She still didn't look all that bright to Anya, but what could you tell just by looking? She looked back to Vasilii. "So, are you planning to be her Doctor Watson?"

"Why not?"

"Because you have the engine system for an airplane to design. Which is much more important than following her around while she comments on the strange thing the dog did in the night."

It was, too. The drawback to dirigibles is simple. They are big. Very big and very fragile. Big makes them expensive and fragile means they rarely last long enough to pay for their construction, as proven by the loss of both the *Czarina Evdokia* and the *Prince Alexi*. Czarist Russia needed to transition from dirigibles to fixed-wing aircraft as soon as possible. And in spite of Bernie's Dodge, internal combustion engine development kept running into quality control issues. Well, materials issues.

"I can do that too," Vasilii insisted. And the truth was that Vasilii didn't have to do anything he didn't want to. He was rich enough to sit on his butt for the next twenty years and never do a lick of work, so Anya let it go.

Anya wrote a quick note. "Take this to Damir, and he will get you set up."

* * *

Damir got them set up, including not just the meal card, but an account at the commissary represented by another card with her name on it and an amount that frankly staggered Miroslava.

Then they went to dinner in the cafeteria. Miroslava copied Vasilii's selections, and copied his use of the up-time designed flatware. It wasn't until they were seated and talking that he realized that Miroslava didn't realize she could choose other options than he did.

Vasilii ate his borscht and considered the case. "We need to get another bullet to check against the one we found in the wall."

"How will you find the gun it was fired from? There are a lot of guns in Ufa."

"We have a suspect," Vasilii said. "Well, Vera says her husband suspects a sniper. Which would fit with the copper-jacketed rounds."

"Who?"

"I don't know his name. We'll go see Vera tomorrow and ask."

* * *

Back in Vasilii's rooms after they had both showered, Vasilii worked at his desk while Miroslava went around and cleaned the room. The Ufa Dacha had electricity, but lacked lightbulbs, so they used oil lamps after sunset. And Vasilii's drafting table had a set of three lamps with mirrors so that the surface was well lit. It also tilted as needed, and Vasilii used bits of gum to hold the sheets in place as he worked.

In just a few minutes Miroslava had Vasilii's rooms in excellent order with everything put away. Vasilii worked for two hours on the designs and after a while Miroslava went over to watch him trying to figure out what he was doing. He was using an abacus, not because he didn't have an adding machine. He did. And a slide rule. But he was used to the abacus. He'd used it since he was a kid. The other things were new, so what could be done on the abacus, he did that way.

He expected Miroslava to ask him what he was doing but she didn't say a word while he worked.

She waited until he was finished, then he asked her, "Which side of the bed do you want?"

"You take your side. I will take the other."

He shrugged and did so, blowing out the lamps on his way to bed. Then Miroslava took off her robe, folded it onto a chair, then stood before him nude.

"You don't have to do that." He stuttered looking away.

"You bought my contract. Is there something wrong with me?" Miroslava's confidence in her attractiveness was a mile wide and half an inch deep. She'd been told for most of her life that the only reason for keeping a freak like her alive was because she was beautiful. She took great pride in her appearance, but it was more than that. Her attractiveness, her sex appeal, were issues of life and death. To be found unattractive was to be found dead in a ditch.

And the owner of her contract was looking away from her.

"No, it's not that. You're beautiful." He glanced down. Miroslava followed his gaze and saw that at least a part of him was interested. "I want to, but you don't have to."

"You own my contract." She reached into her bag, and pulled out a condom. "Besides, I like it. It feels good." Then she climbed into bed next to him.

Location: Factory of Stefan Andreevich Ruzukov
Date: April 21, 1637, 8:30 AM

Miroslava considered Vasilii as they walked. He wasn't inexperienced, but could benefit from some training. Of course, experience had taught her that attempting to tell men how to have sex was difficult to do without giving them offense, and could be dangerous, depending on the man. Breakfast that morning was scrambled eggs, warm black bread with butter, and cedar nut and black currant jam, all she could eat, which made it the best meal she'd eaten this year.

She wasn't wearing her work clothes today. She was wearing her normal clothes. They were undyed broadcloth. A skirt, belted, and a blouse, covered with a cloak. The ground was starting to thaw in the morning sun, so her shoes were leaking a bit and her feet were cold and wet. Which they had been all winter.

They opened the door to the building, to see workmen busily putting the shop back together. It still wasn't back in production yet, but they were getting there. A workman directed them to an office. Once they were in and the door closed, the amount of noise was much less.

"Good morning, Stefan," Vasilii said. "Your wife asked me to look into the murder of Fiana."

"She told me. What have you found?" Stefan was a big man, tall and broad with muscles on his muscles. He was swathed in linen bandages holding his left arm in place. He also had bandages on his head, but none of them seemed to keep him from working. Or maybe they did. He was here, after all, not out in the work room.

"The bullet that killed her," Vasilii said.

Miroslava said nothing, because for a woman of her class, to speak out in public was to invite a beating. And though she was coming to trust Vasilii, she didn't trust him fully yet. And she didn't trust the big blacksmith at all.

"What good is that?"

"If we find the gun that fired it, we can prove that it was the gun."

"How?" That led to a discussion of rifling, ballistic lands and grooves, and fingerprints that Miroslava took in like water to a dying plant. The notion that everything was unique, and knowing all the features of something let you tell it from all the others, fit her view of the world perfectly.

"I can give you the person who did the shooting if you can prove it. Or, at least, my workman can." He called out and the door was opened. A much smaller man stood in it. "Petr, find Egor and send him in."

It took a few minutes, while Vasilii asked Stefan about how the work was coming, and Stefan explained what they were doing and why. Then Egor came in.

Miroslava recognized Egor, but he didn't even notice her. Miroslava wasn't unattractive, but when not in her work clothing, and not wearing the white makeup and the bright red lip gloss, she looked a lot different. Her regular clothes did more to hide her figure than to show it.

Egor gave them Feliks Pavlovich's name, and that seemed wrong to Miroslava. She wasn't quite sure why, but there was something wrong. Not about what he said happened in the club, but about what he assumed happened later. It didn't quite fit with what she knew about Feliks, but she wasn't sure how.

Location: Ufa Kremlin, Barracks Area

Captain Pushka Lazarivich Anosov wasn't happy to see them. "Feliks is a good soldier and an excellent shot. What proof do you have?" A repeat of the explanation of ballistics, plus the invoking of Anya and Bernie Zeppi still didn't provide the rifle's release. But they did get the commander's assurance that the AK4.7 sniper rifle would be locked up.

Location: Ufa Kremlin, Apartments of Bernie Zeppi

Bernie was kissing Natasha when the knock came. Vladimir had only just left and they had hoped for a few minutes of privacy.

They looked at each other, shook their heads, and said, in unison, "Every single time."

Then Bernie opened the door. "Vasilii? What are you doing here and why are you trying to ruin my love life?"

Vasilii blinked, then saw Natasha and blushed. Natasha was wearing makeup, but not the white pancake makeup that was popular in Moscow before the Ring of Fire. She and the czarina now wore makeup in the up-timer style, mostly gathered from magazines located in Grantville.

Miroslava looked at the pink cheeks and slightly smudged subdued red of the Princess' lip gloss and wondered how she could get ahold of makeup like that. It looked like she wasn't wearing makeup at all, but was just naturally beautiful. Or at least that was what Miroslava thought it would look like, if it hadn't just been smudged.

"I need you to get Czar Mikhail to issue a warrant for the rifle of Feliks Pavlovich."

Bernie looked at Natasha and sighed. "Come in and tell us all about it. The mood is ruined anyway."

Telling all about it took a while, and involved introducing and explaining Miroslava, which was complicated by the fact that the assumption everyone made wasn't totally inaccurate. It was simply not all of it. "She's the one who figured out where the bullet was. And where the shooter was, as well."

That led to more conversation and Bernie pointing out, "You need to teach her to read. With her memory, there's a good chance she'll learn fast."

It took almost two hours, and the conclusion was that, for this instance, they would get an order from the czar, but they also needed to come up with a way for the not yet formed judiciary to issue warrants in the czar's name for the collecting of evidence, and some way of assuring that the evidence would be returned to its rightful owner.

And even at that, Czar Mikhail was busy. They wouldn't be getting the warrant until tomorrow.

Gorg Huff & Paula Goodlett

CHAPTER 4— FORENSICS AREN'T PERFECT

Location: Ufa Dacha, Work Area
Date: April 22, 1637

The firing rig was a tank of water that was based on something Bernie had seen in a movie sometime before the Ring of Fire. It was ten feet long, four feet deep and four feet wide. The gun was clamped in place and fired at an angle that should be deep enough so that the bullet wouldn't deflect off the surface of the water but shallow enough so that it would have the full ten-foot length of the tank to slow in.

The bullet was then collected from the bottom of the tank and comparison could be done.

Miroslava was convinced that the bullets wouldn't match.

They did.

"Your test is wrong."

So they tested other rifles, pistols, all sorts of things. The other rifles, even other rifles that were supposedly the same as Feliks' didn't match, and Feliks' rifle did.

"I'm sorry, Miroslava, but the evidence is clear," Vasilii said

"No. Something is wrong," Miroslava insisted.

In spite of which, Feliks was taken into custody, and his rifle taken into evidence. Feliks wasn't even a *dvoriane*, but he was a *streltzi*. That made arresting him for the murder of a bar girl something that wouldn't happen back in Moscow. And something that the local cop commander was less than thrilled to be doing.

Location: Cells in the Ufa Kremlin
Date: April 22, 8 PM

"I'm going to enjoy this," Petr said, smiling and cracking his knuckles. Actually, he was mostly bored. They had the little bastard for the murder, sure enough, but the commander wanted everything in order and ready for the magistrate.

It was Petr's job to get a confession. He would too. Looking at this bastard, Petr already knew he could get him to admit to murdering his mother back in Moscow.

He did. It took a surprising four hours, the loss of two of Feliks' teeth and his nose was never going to look the same.

Not that that would matter. This bastard would be hanging from a gibbet before the bruises healed.

Location: Alley Beside The Happy Bottom
Date: April 23, 1637, 3 AM

Marina was saying good night to Dominika who was her special friend, the same thing she'd been doing when Fiana was killed. Marina was fond of Dominika. She was a chubby girl with freckles, blue eyes, and curly red hair. She liked Dominika in a way that she didn't when it came to men. Not even Karol, who was the father of her child—she thought— and who'd been a nice man and treated her well until his death in the battle of the field eleven days ago. Little Larisa Karolevna Chernoff didn't get to meet him. She went into labor about the same time that Karol went into combat, and Marina wasn't at all sure whether Larisa was born first, or Karol died first.

For the first two days after the battle, she stayed in Karol's apartment, then the bastard landlord threw her out, even though Karol had paid for the month. But it didn't matter. There was no one to take up her cause. So on the third day after Karol died, she ended up back here. Madam Drozdov took her in, and after another two days, put her to work carrying drinks. She'd be dancing in another month, and she didn't have any choice at all. Little Larisa needed a roof over her head, and so did Marina.

So she was here in the cold saying good night to Dominika. She kissed her friend on the cheek, then waved as Dominika walked off into the night.

Then the crossbow bolt hit her, and she screamed. There was a stick sticking out of her belly and she fell to the ground. The bolt struck the ground, and Marina screamed again, then fainted.

✳ ✳ ✳

Anatoly looked at Marina, and thought, *Not again.* Then he screamed at Dariya to run and get the watch, and he went to see about Marina. She was alive, but seeing the wound Anatoly figured that would change in a few days, or a few weeks. The arrow went in near her belly button. It almost had to have cut the intestine. A part of him wanted to cut her throat just to save her the pain. But not here. Not in Ufa, where the great and the mighty might decide it was murder, not mercy.

Here, Marina would just have to suffer.

In passing, he wondered how long her baby would live, but that wasn't his business.

They were still getting her back into the club when the cops showed up, in the person of Pavel Borisovich.

"Again? What is it with your girls, Anatoly?"

"Not my girls. Like I said before, I just work here. And besides Marina wasn't dancing. She just served drinks. At least recently."

✳ ✳ ✳

Pavel considered the situation. There wasn't likely much they could do for the girl, but if anyone could, it would be Doctor Tami. And Pavel knew someone who could probably get her here.

Pavel couldn't write. He grabbed one of the girls. "What's your name?"

"Roksana," the girl admitted, like she was afraid he was going to arrest her if she didn't give the name he wanted.

"Do you know where the Ufa Dacha is?" She should. The compound was almost as big as the Kremlin and located on prime real estate.

"Da."

"You run to the Dacha and ask for Miroslava. She's staying with Vasilii Lyapunov." He shook her to get her attention. "As soon as you get to her, tell her what happened here and see if she can get a doctor for Marina."

He turned her around and slapped her bottom. "Now, go."

* * *

Roksana ran, hating her luck. Marina had a protector to take care of her, or did until he was killed. Now Miroslava had a protector, and all Roksana ever got was bastards like that cop, slapping her ass and ordering her around.

It didn't take her all that long. Ufa wasn't a big place even yet. It was not even as big as Nizhny Novgorod, much less Moscow. The people who came here came in three categories: people who had no choice because they were running from something back home; people looking for the main chance who figured that now was their best chance to get rich—Roksana was part of that second category—and the noble ones who came to Ufa to serve the czar or change the world.

The Dacha was full of that third kind of people. The suckers. Marina and Miroslava found suckers. Why couldn't she?

She got to the gate, which had a guard. "I need to talk to Miroslava. She's with Vasilii something," she panted, trying to get her breath back and remember the man's family name. "Lyapunov, that's it. Lyapunov."

As it happened, the guard knew exactly who she was talking about. Vasilii's new doxy was the talk of the Dacha. "I know who you mean, but she's probably snuggled up close to Master

Lyapunov, the lucky bastard. So why should I interrupt their fun for you?"

"Marina got shot with a crossbow, and the cop sent me to tell her and Vasilii, and get a doctor."

At that point the guard called an escort and sent her in. They still weren't going to let just anyone wander around the Dacha in the middle of the night.

* * *

Miroslava woke as soon as the pounding started, and got up to see. She put on Vasilii's robe. He'd promised to get her one, but they hadn't gotten around to it. They hadn't gotten around to a lot of things.

Vasilii was still waking up when she called through the door, "Who is it?" In Miroslava's rather extensive experience, you didn't open your door in the middle of the night unless you wanted to get beaten, robbed, raped, or all three.

It was her voice, not the knocking, that got Vasilii sitting up in bed.

"Miroslava, it's Roksana. Marina's been shot with a crossbow, and the cop sent me to get you so you could get her a doctor."

"Let her in," Vasilii said, reaching onto the bedside table for a striker. He lifted the chimney on the lamp, and used the striker to light it, still naked except for the blanket.

Miroslava opened the door and Roksana came in, followed by a large man whose tunic showed the brightly colored Gorchakov crest.

With the blanket wrapped around him, Vasilii came over. "You can leave the young lady here, Ivan. We need you to send a message to Tami Simmons, or if not Tami, one of her doctor trainees to meet us here. I know where to take them."

The guard nodded and ran off.

Miroslava got the story out of Roksana, while she and Vasilii got dressed. Roksana made no bones about giving Vasilii a good once over as he was putting on his pants.

Miroslava was a bit surprised by her resentment of that once over. She didn't like it. She was definitely feeling possessive of Vasilii.

* * *

On their way back to The Happy Bottom, Vasilii asked about Marina. Miroslava had him talk to Roksana because something was distracting her. It had to do with the night that Fiana was killed, but she couldn't put it together.

"She's gone into her weirdness," Roksana told Vasilii. "She's never been all there, as long as I've known her. It makes no sense her and Marina being so lucky."

"How are they lucky?" Vasilii asked.

"You. Well, you and that rich guy Marina had."

"What rich guy?"

"Karol Karolivich. She was pregnant and he took care of her, even promised to acknowledge it." Roksana shrugged. "Of course, he got himself killed in the battle the same day the kid was born. But at least she had him while she was fat."

The conversations continued while they made their way to The Happy Bottom. Tami, with Esim, a Tatar doctor who was now working with her and studying surgery, looked Marina over.

"The odds aren't good. We have some of the Chlometh, but not that much." Chlometh was the name in Russia for the artificial antibiotics developed in Grantville and shared with the world. About one person in twenty-five thousand had a fatal allergic reaction to it, but in a case like Marina's that wasn't even worth consideration. The issue was that they were ten days past a major battle with massive casualties and lots of infections. Their stock of the drug was pretty much used up. And in spite of the czar's reforms and the new constitution, there were a lot of people of higher status than a bar girl waiting for the next dose of the stuff to come out of the chemistry lab.

Still, Tami insisted that she be taken to the Kremlin hospice, so that they could type her blood and maybe do surgery to sew up the cuts in her intestines, and clean out the wound. That would at least give her a better chance of fighting off the infection on her own.

* * *

As they watched Tami, Esim, and the stretcher bearers leave with Marina, Miroslava said, "It was the same man."

"What was the same man?" Vasilii asked. "No . . . you can't mean that Marina and Fiana were shot by the same man. We have the man who shot Fiana. He's locked up in the cells in the Kremlin. He can't have shot Marina."

"Not him. He didn't do—" She stopped in mid-sentence, looked down the alley, then looked at the bloodstain on the ground where Marina's blood darkened the muddy ground, looked at the place where Vasilii's chalk marks were fading, and then she turned and started walking.

"What?" Vasilii waited a moment, then ran after her. She walked down the block, past the first block to the second, then she turned and stood, looking back at the side door of The Happy Bottom. She pointed. And, as best he could, Vasilii followed her finger. She moved her finger, but just a fraction of an inch, then moved it back. Now Vasilii got it. She was pointing at the two targets. He tried it. His finger moved a bit more than hers, but not much. He moved behind her, tried again. No, his finger was still moving farther. "What is it, Miroslava?"

"He was shooting at Marina both times."

"Can't be. They were too far apart, even from this distance."

She turned and looked at him, and he demonstrated. She shook her head. "Not where Marina was tonight when she was shot. Where she was when *Fiana* was shot."

Vasilii suddenly felt like an idiot. It was obvious now that she said it. Something he should have seen from the beginning. He remembered a scene from one of the books he'd read, where someone he didn't remember used toy soldiers to recreate a crime scene. He would do that as soon as they got back home.

In the meantime, it was looking like Miroslava was right about who shot Fiana, but that couldn't be. It would mean that two rifles had the same rifling and that couldn't happen.

Besides, who had a motive for killing Marina?

Location: Ufa Kremlin, Hospice
Date: April 23, 1637, 10 AM

Dominika was sitting at Marina's bedside with the baby. Partly because she was Marina's friend, but partly to get the baby out of The Happy Bottom and Madam Drozdov's sight. And, maybe, if she was lucky, find someone to feed the little girl. She couldn't. Dominika was careful. She'd never been pregnant, and didn't intend to be.

The curtain opened and Miroslava and her patron came in. Dominika didn't much like Miroslava. Miroslava was strange, and strange girls meant trouble sooner or later.

"Is she awake?" Miroslava asked.

"No, not yet. And I don't know what to do about the baby."

"I'm not sure Tami will want her breastfeeding the baby if she's on drugs to keep her asleep," Vasilii offered.

"The baby needs to eat. She's only eighteen days old."

"Born on the day of the battle?" Vasilii asked.

"Yes. Her father, Karol Karolivich Chernoff, died in the battle."

"I think I met him once or twice," Vasilii said. The baby chose then to wake up and start crying. She was hungry.

Vasilii went for a nurse's aide to seek out a wetnurse. There were such available, not to mention goat's milk, but both were expensive.

Vasilii got stuck with the bill. Vasilii was well off, but this little adventure was getting expensive.

Finally, about an hour later, the baby fed and asleep again, Vasilii got to ask his question, if indirectly. "Do you know why anyone would want to kill Marina?"

"No. There might have been, but Karol died, so he didn't legitimize little Larisa Karolevna."

"Tell me about that."

Dominika started talking. She told them the story of Karol and Marina from Marina's point of view and finished with: "He never signed the papers. He was a nice guy even if he was a *Deti Boyar*. He would have if he'd lived through the battle, even though she turned out to be a daughter rather than a son." Dominika looked sadly at the little girl.

Vasilii nodded. "I wonder how his family responded when they got the news. . . ?"

"They ordered Marina killed," Miroslava said, like he was an idiot.

"You may well be right, Miroslava. But how are we going to prove it?"

"Why do we have to?"

That stopped Vasilii. He didn't know why they had to prove it. That was just how all the mysteries ended, with the clever detective finding proof or getting a confession. "Well," Vasilii said thoughtfully, "we want the guilty person punished."

"Well, if you want someone punished, Feliks is probably going to hang. He's not the one who did it, but he can be punished for it," Miroslava said.

"Speaking of which, we probably ought to go talk to Pavel and see about having a talk with Feliks. I still want to know how Fiana got shot with his rifle. Maybe he shot her while aiming for Marina."

"He's supposed to be a good shot," Miroslava said doubtfully.

"What about Marina?" Dominika asked. "Is she going to be all right?"

Miroslava said, "And even if he was paid to kill Marina and missed, he didn't shoot her with a crossbow. He's locked up in the cells in the Kremlin."

"What about Marina?" Dominika asked again, sounding like she was on the edge of hysteria. "Who's going to take care of the baby if she dies? I can't pay for a wet nurse."

"Calm down," Vasilii said. "Take a breath, and let's think this through. It may be that the baby at least has some claim on Karol's money, or at least support. I will look into it for you. In the meantime, they are both safe here."

Location: Cells, Ufa Kremlin
Date: April 23, 1637, 1 PM

After lunch at the Dacha, they went to the Kremlin to see Feliks. What they found was almost enough to shock Miroslava, and more than enough to shock Vasilii. Feliks was huddled in a corner of the cell. There were three other men in the ten by fifteen wooden room. It had an unglazed hole in the wall near the ceiling which let in a little light. The temperature in the room was above freezing. You could tell that by the unfrozen urine and crap in a bucket in a corner. But it wasn't much above freezing, even though the temperature outside was in the mid-forties. Feliks' formerly good clothing was torn and filthy with blood and worse things. His face was a mass of bruises, and he was breathing through his mouth because he couldn't breathe through his thoroughly broken nose. One fingernail was missing, little finger of his left hand.

Vasilii, holding a handkerchief over his nose, said to the guard, "Pull him out of there. We need to ask him some questions."

The guard grinned a gap tooth grin, and said, "We already did. He's admitted to killing the girl. Not so tough without that long gun, he's not."

Vasilii didn't doubt it. Looking at the formerly somewhat arrogant sniper, huddled crying in a corner, Vasilii imagined that he would admit murdering the czar if Mikhail was standing hale and hearty right in front of him while he did the admitting.

In his mystery books there were coerced confessions, and the books all agreed that they were a bad thing. That was, or had been until this moment, one of many things in those books that Vasilii willingly suspended his disbelief about. But Vasilii only suspended it. If asked yesterday or five minutes ago about the use of torture to get a confession, Vasilii would have said it was a necessary evil in a world that lacked the tech for proper forensic analysis. Now, in his gut, Vasilii understood. This didn't get you truth. It got you whatever the questioner wanted to hear.

He looked at the grinning guard and realized something else. Nothing Vasilii could say would convince this basically good man that torture was a bad thing.

He sighed. "I don't doubt that he admitted killing her. But we have some other questions to ask, and I don't think we will need torture to get our answers."

He looked over at Miroslava. She was looking around, a slight frown on her face. She sniffed the air. Shook her head. Vasili knew that look. It was Miroslava deciding not to say anything. Even this soon there were a couple of things that Vasilii understood about Miroslava. One was that she wasn't good at dealing with people, and the other was that she knew it. Her first instinct was to blurt out everything, but some very hard knocks had trained her over the years to not speak. That muzzle worked most of the time, except when she was excited or upset. And the least little contradiction would put the muzzle back in place. "What is it, Miroslava?"

Miroslava looked at him, and he nodded reassurance, so she said, "If they don't clean this place, we're going to have a slow plague flare up in Ufa."

"Slow plague" was the Russian name for a cholera outbreak. That happened in Moscow every spring. It happened in other cities as well, and Bernie Zeppi was sort of famous for having decreased its severity in Moscow for years.

Vasilii knew about the slow plague. He'd had an older sister once. He'd loved her madly when he was six and she was ten. She died of the slow plague when she was eleven.

He turned to the guard. "You will want to get some lye soap and put the prisoners to work cleaning this place."

The cop's expression was a combination of doubt and resentment, barely held in check by Vasilii's rank. Vasilii continued, "You want to already be at the cleaning when Tami Simmons comes to look at this place. And you really don't want to find out how Bernie Zeppi is going to react if there is a slow plague outbreak here and it's traced back to this place."

Now the cop was just looking scared.

"Meanwhile, drag Feliks out and clean him . . ." Vasilii considered. "No. Come to think of it, I'm going to want to take him to the hospice."

"He's in jail. You can't just take him out because you decide it," the man insisted belligerently.

"You're right. We'll go see the colonel."

* * *

Two hours later, they interviewed Feliks as he was lying in a bed in the hospice. One arm was manacled to the side of the bed, and a bored Pavel was sitting there watching. His punishment for not keeping Vasilii out of the colonel's way.

"Yes, I did it. You can hang me. Just don't send me back there," Feliks whimpered before Vasilii could ask him anything.

"Why did you do it?"

"I was jealous, just like you said."

"Jealous of Marina?"

"Marina? Who's Marina?"

"The girl—" Vasilii started, but Miroslava grabbed his arm.

"Let me ask," Miroslava insisted.

Vasilii looked at her, stood up from the chair, and offered it to her.

Pavel looked at Vasilii, and grinned. The grin said, in the up-timer phrase that Vasilii had read in one of his mysteries, "You are so pussy whipped."

Vasilii shrugged his agreement while Miroslava started asking questions.

"Where was Fiana standing when you shot her?"

"I don't know?"

"How can you not know if you shot her?"

"I . . . I . . . She was in the alley."

"Very good. She was in the alley. Where in the alley?"

"What do you mean? She was in the alley. I shot her. Now you can hang me."

"Was she closer to you than the door?"

"Yes, yes, she was closer."

As Miroslava, Vasilii, and Pavel all knew perfectly well, the door was closer to the shooter than Fiana was. Until now, Pavel had been watching this whole procedure with a mixture of resentment and boredom, with a bit of amusement thrown in. Now that boredom was gone. His eyes sharpened, and he paid careful attention.

Vasilii pulled a notepad from his breast pocket. Like better than half the workers in the Dacha of whatever rank, Vasilii had pockets sewn into his tunic. The one on the left breast contained a small wooden board that had twenty small sheets of paper clamped to it. It also contained a wooden pencil with a real graphite and clay lead. They'd been being made in Moscow for over two years when the czar escaped. They still weren't being made in Ufa, but a lot of them were "smuggled" to Kazan and Ufa. They were what Bernie called "seventeenth-century geek chic." Almost a badge of honor among the Dacha crowd.

Now Vasilii took out his notepad and pencil and started taking careful notes as Miroslava asked her questions.

It took awhile because Miroslava was careful of her questions. It wasn't until well into the interview that Vasilii realized why she was being so careful. She was working very hard to see that none of her questions told Feliks what sort of answer she wanted, and that her responses to his answers didn't tell him if he'd said what she wanted or not. That was very hard to do and Miroslava didn't always manage it.

But she asked him who was in the alley, where everyone was standing, how he could see, inadvertently giving away that there was a lamp. Where the lamp was. "Over the door." Something must have shown in one of their expressions, because he quickly corrected himself. "No, no, someone was carrying it."

"Who?"

"One of the girls. I don't remember which."

And on and on, like that. Every detail. Vasilii didn't understand how she could keep all the details straight as she asked her questions.

It was conclusive. Feliks wasn't in the alley. There were too many things he didn't know, things that he couldn't get wrong if he'd been there, looking down the sights of his rifle.

"Tell me about your gun."

"My rifle?"

"Yes. I'm sorry, Feliks. That's right. Guns and rifles aren't exactly the same. How are they different?"

"Rifles have rifling," Feliks said, looking resentfully at Vasilii, then casting a frightened glance at Pavel, who was still watching from across the room.

"Yes. That's true, but that's not what I want to know. Can you shoot other rifles?"

"I can shoot anything," Feliks said, forgetting for a moment his situation in his pride at his marksmanship.

"Can anyone shoot your rifle?"

"Not as well as me."

"Is that just because you're a good shot, or are there other reasons?"

"Mostly it's because I'm a good shot. I've hunted all my life. But, yes, there are things about Nadia that only I know."

Nadia, as they all knew by now, was Feliks' name for his sniper rifle. It was a custom-made single-shot with a forty-seven inch barrel. It was converted from a flintlock to a cap lock in 1636, and had cost Feliks twenty-five rubles.

"Tell me about Nadia. What makes her special? What makes her different from other rifles?"

"Well, she has her name carved on the butt stock, and mine carved on the fore-end." The fore-end was the wooden piece on the barrel forward of the action. In the case of Nadia, it was a pump. When pushed forward, it ejected the spent chamber, and when pulled back toward the action, it seated the new chamber and cocked the hammer, leaving the rifle ready to fire. "She sticks a little on the push, so you really have to jerk it out. But it pulls back smooth." He considered. "And the front sight's bent just a touch. You almost wouldn't notice it, but I correct for it."

"How do you correct for it?"

"I don't aim over the site, but just to the right of it. It's like correcting for windage, but it's consistent."

Vasilii looked over at Pavel at that, thinking *Well now we know why it was Fiana who was hit the first night, not Marina.*

Pavel looked back sourly. Yes, it was true. They now knew that Feliks didn't kill Fiana, or apparently anyone he wasn't supposed to, but that wasn't news to make his colonel happy, especially since they didn't have an actual murderer to replace him.

He jerked a thumb at the door to the ward.

* * *

"You enjoy making my life miserable don't you, Vasilii?" Pavel hissed in disgust after they were out of the ward. By now he knew Vasilii well enough to know that he could get away with the complaint. "The colonel's going to be pissed, and he can't take it out on you, so he's going to take it out on me."

Vasilii grinned. "Well, there are things I enjoy more, Pavel, but I will admit it doesn't bother me much." Then Vasilii's face went calm, almost grim. "Not nearly as much as I am bothered by the fact that an innocent man was tortured and might well have been hung."

"And why did we have him in the first place? Who pointed us at him, told us his motives, and proved that it was his gun that did the deed? What were we supposed to think? With all due respect, you're the one who got him tortured and almost hung. It was your girl in there that showed he didn't do it. And even now it's going to be hard to get the colonel to let him go. We have his confession, after all, and maybe he made up the stuff he told us in there, trying to get out of hanging.

"You think my colonel is going to believe that a professional torturer was fooled, and your doxy figured it out?" Pavel held up a hand. "I think she's right, but I know her. My colonel doesn't.

"Look, I can keep him here, not back in the cells. But he's not leaving the Dacha until you find us someone to replace him with."

"Why me?" Vasilii complained. "You're the cop."

"What do I know about detecting? You invited yourself onto this investigation, so you can figure it out."

* * *

Back in the ward, Miroslava was finished with her questioning. Well, almost finished. There was one more thing she needed to know, but she couldn't figure out how to ask it without letting Feliks know that she knew he didn't do it. So she told him. "You didn't do it, Feliks. You couldn't have. You don't know enough about how the crime was committed."

"But I admitted it."

"Yes, you admitted it, but we both know you just did that so that the pain would stop. Don't feel bad. Anyone will say untrue things if you hurt them bad enough. I hate to say anything untrue, but I've done it when I was hurt, just like you did. And I wasn't hurt nearly as much as you were."

"Are they going to torture me again?"

"I don't know. I will try to stop them, and Vasilii will too, I think. But I don't know if it will work. Now, listen to me,

Feliks. I need to know how someone could have gotten your rifle."

"No one could. I always have it with me."

"You didn't have it with you in the club," Miroslava said.

"No. I left it in the cloakroom, just like always. And when we got thrown out, I was so drunk I just went back to the barracks and fell on my bunk. But it was right there when I went back to get it the next morning. My rifle, my pistol, all my stuff. Even my money . . .

"Wait a minute. There was a fired chamber in my bandolier. I didn't think much of it at the time. I usually like to have them all loaded and ready to go, but sometimes I forget."

"You went back the next morning? How did you get in?"

"I banged on the door, and the fat girl opened it. I gave her my ticket and she gave me my stuff."

"Thank you, Feliks. I need to ask the fat girl some questions now."

✳ ✳ ✳

The fat girl was Marina. The fatness was left over from her pregnancy and the good food she'd had during it. As it happened, Marina was in the same hospice, next ward over.

Miroslava was halfway there when she realized that Marina wasn't going to tell "the weird girl" anything, not unless someone of importance was right there to make her.

She collected Vasilii and Pavel, then went to ask Marina about the gun. Miroslava tried to use the same technique of no leading questions that she'd used with Feliks, but Marina didn't remember anything. She was in pain and was on opium, which made the questioning more difficult. Also, Dominika wanted to know what Vasilii had found out about the baby.

"I'm sorry. I haven't had time to find out."

It took some coaxing and a leading question. "The morning after Fiana was killed, did anyone knock on the doors?"

"I don't know. Maybe. I was tired."

"What did they want?"

"His stuff."

"Whose stuff?"

"That short, ugly sniper. He wanted his precious rifle. My stomach hurts. My breasts hurt. I need to feed Larisa. She's been so good."

"Did you give him his rifle?"

"Who?"

"The person who banged on the door, the one who woke you up."

"Oh, him. Yeah. He had the ticket, and his guns and overcoat were right there."

Miroslava looked at Pavel. "Which means for Feliks to have killed Fiana with Nadia, he would have had to have gotten into the cloakroom at The Happy Bottom before the murder. Gotten back into the cloakroom after the murder to put it back. Then come back the next morning to collect it from Marina."

Pavel nodded, looking disgusted. "I will talk to the colonel."

"Wait a moment, I just had a thought," Vasilii said. "One of the things that happens a lot in murder mysteries."

Pavel groaned, and Miroslava grinned.

"No, really. This might be important." Vasilii didn't whine but there was a bit of a pleading note in his voice. "Sometimes they leave the innocent guy in jail because they don't want the guilty one to find out that he's still being hunted. Right now, everyone knows that Feliks is the suspect in the murder of Fiana, and we don't have a suspect in the attempted murder of Marina. No one knows that we know that Marina was the target both times."

There were twin gasps at that point, one rather weak from Marina in the bed, and another, louder, from Dominika.

Pavel actually laughed at that, and Vasilii turned a bit red. "I probably should have waited until we were alone to mention that, shouldn't I?"

"Yes, Miss Marple, you probably should have," Pavel said. He'd been being lectured on the exploits of Miss Marple,

Inspector Poirot, Sherlock Holmes, and so on for the last couple of days, and he was pretty sure that he had the right character. She wasn't a police person, just an amateur sleuth like Vasilii wanted to be. And—he looked over at Miroslava— like Miroslava actually was.

"You have to protect Marina," Dominika said.

"You have to protect my baby," Marina said at the same time.

"You're safe here for the moment. You're in the middle of the Ufa Kremlin," Pavel said. Then, at their expressions added, "I will get an extra guard up here. It won't take long. Meantime, you girls listen to me and listen good. Anyone you tell about what we were just saying might tell the murderer and let him get away. And until we catch him, you're not safe. So keep your mouths shut."

Pavel can do a very credible menacing, Vasilii thought as both girls were caught between cringing away from him and clinging to him.

* * *

Once outside, Vasilii whispered, "We have too much to do and not enough people to do it. First, we need to go to The Happy Bottom and find out how the rifle got from the cloakroom to that alley. At the same time, we need to get more guards on the girls." He hooked a thumb at the ward they'd just left. "And we need to find out about that baby. I think the baby is the key to all this."

"You may be right, but you have to go with Miroslava to The Happy Bottom because if you aren't there, no one is going to listen to her or answer any of her questions," Pavel said. Miroslava nodded her complete agreement.

Pavel continued. "I will talk to my colonel, get some men up here just in case, and I will also ask him to find out about Marina's bastard."

Gorg Huff & Paula Goodlett

CHAPTER 5—ABOVE MY PAY GRADE

Location: Office of the Cop Commander, Ufa Kremlin
Date: April 23, 1637, 4:30 PM

Pavel waited until the door to the colonel's office was closed before he started explaining.

Colonel Evgeny Ivanovich Aslonav wasn't in a very good position. His family was among the *dvoriane*, but at the very bottom end of it. Technically, he out ranked a *streltzi*, but in any other circumstances he would be a lieutenant, not a colonel in command of twenty or thirty *streltzi* cops, not the entire police force for what had just become the capital of Russia. He was out of his depth, not just in terms of rank and political connections, but in terms of ability.

And worst of all, he knew it.

Almost in desperation, but hiding it fairly well, he asked, "What do you think we should do, Pavel?"

"I think we need to keep Marina and her bastard safe, sir," Pavel said. "If someone is going to this much trouble over them, and it's not just a madman, they are more important than we know. And, sir, we need to go to the clerk's office and find out what, if anything, Karol Karolivich Chernoff did about the child. And, sir, for that we need your rank."

"All right. But you're going with me, and you're going to explain what we need."

* * *

Iosef Ufukivich Bortnik looked over as the door opened. He was grabbing his coat. It was late April, but the evenings were still chilly. Seeing who was there, he put his coat back on the hook.

"Yes, Colonel. What can I do for you?"

The colonel waved at the man, who stepped forward. "We need you to look up Captain Karol Karolivich Chernoff and find out what, if any, provision he made for the child carried by his mistress, Marina."

"That again?"

"Who else asked you for that information?" Pavel asked, not waiting for the colonel's permission.

The clerk looked at the colonel, and Colonel Evgeny Ivanovich Aslonav showed his rank. "Answer the question!" he growled like a hungry tiger.

"Sure, no problems. It's not a secret. A man came in and asked about anything on Karol. He was pleased about finding out that Karol had claimed the child while it was still in the womb. With Karol dead, when the baby is born, it will be the ranking Chernoff in the czar's ranks. Not that that's going to stand. The son of a club girl. Major embarrassment for the family, though."

Pavel looked at the clerk, then at his boss, and he felt a smile on his face. "Please mark in your records that Lady Larisa Karolevna Chernoff was born on the day of the battle. According to all reports, some two hours before her father died defending Ufa. And you might want to send a note to Czar Mikhail, telling him that he still has a member of the Chernoff clan in his ranks to give the Chernoff lands to when we win this thing."

"A bar girl's bastard daughter? You have to be joking."

"No, he doesn't have to be joking. In fact, he's not joking at all. Make your note Mister . . . Just what is your name?"

"Iosif Ufukivich Bortnik, sir. But a lot of the *Deti Boyars* aren't going to be happy, and I don't think it's even legal."

"Equal protection under the law," said Colonel Aslonav. "It's the very first effective clause of the new constitution. 'All persons residing in the Empire of Russia shall have equal protection under the law.' So she has just as much right to inherit as anyone else, and he named her his heir. As to how the nobles are going to feel about it, the only one who is going to matter in this is Czar Mikhail, and he's probably going to be thrilled."

Colonel Aslonav looked at Pavel. "Are you done here, Sergeant?"

"Yes, sir. For now."

"Good. Come with me. We are . . . No. You go back to the office. I want around the clock protection on that child, and her mother as well. I have another call to make."

✳ ✳ ✳

The czar had a palace now. It was not even in the Kremlin, but it was only about half built, so every morning he left the royal palace and, accompanied by a squad of cops, he came to the Kremlin to do his work. If he was lucky, he got to go home about seven in the evening. Today wasn't looking to be a lucky day, so when he was informed that Colonel Evgeny Ivanovich Aslonav wanted an urgent word, his first thought was: Colonel who? His second was: I don't have time. His third, though, was: Why would he want an urgent word?

Mikhail tried to remember Colonel Aslonav. He'd met him once, when he appointed him to the command of the city cops, two months after Mikhail got here. And in all the time since there had yet to be a single request for an audience. "Ask him what it's about."

"I did, Sire. He said it had to do with the Chernoff family. That's why I brought it to you."

"All right. Let's hear what the colonel has to say."

As it happened, Colonel Aslonav's assessment of how Czar Mikhail would feel about the news was spot on. Even underestimating it a bit. Mikhail wasn't fond of the family, and he had been fond of Karol. A good kid, young, a bit self-righteous, and not all that bright, but he tried. The boy had tried.

"Thank you, Colonel. Now tell me how this came to your attention."

For the next fifteen minutes Colonel Aslonav briefed the czar on the case of the Happy Bottom Murders, the interest from Vasilii, who the czar did know fairly well, the work he was doing being vitally important for the air force. And the discovery that the murder and the attempted murder were, in all probability, committed by the same man, and that they were about the baby and her mother.

"That means that they were hired done," Mikhail said. "Very well, Colonel. You have done well, and you have my thanks. I want the assassin caught, and I want him caught alive. I want him to be able to testify about who hired him and what they wanted him to do."

Colonel Aslonav swallowed visibly and seemed almost ready to speak, but just nodded.

Czar Mikhail nodded too, and gestured that the interview was over.

Once he was gone, Mikhail shook his head. There didn't seem much chance that the assassin would be caught at all, much less alive and able to talk. Mikhail was a bit disappointed that Aslonav wasn't willing to tell him so. The ability to speak truth to power was important, and apparently not one of Aslonav's talents.

He turned to his secretary. "Find out the status of the baby's mother and see if there's anything else we can do. Talk to Tami Simmons."

Location: The Happy Bottom
Date: April 23, 1637, 4:30 PM

While Pavel went to give the colonel the bad news about their murder suspect, Miroslava and Vasilii went to The Happy Bottom in search of answers about the gun. The club was open for business, though the after-work crowd wasn't there yet, and there wasn't much of a line. One of the girls was on door duty with a bouncer as backup, but Vasilii didn't want to talk to them. At least, not yet.

"I need to have a few words with Madam Drozdov."

The music could be heard in the background. It was loud, with a driving beat, and in American English, apparently a record made from one of the up-timer tapes or CDs.

The door girl still tried to get them to pay the door charge, but Miroslava wasn't having it.

* * *

Elena Drozdov was not having a good week. She was seated behind a polished wood table in a well-padded chair. A Coleman lamp filled the room with light. The walls were whitewashed. There was even a shelf of knickknacks attached to the wall to her right, but she wasn't having a good week.

Murders are bad for business, even if they happen after hours. And with one of her girls dead, two in the hospital, and Miroslava's contract sold, she was short on staff. Besides, having the cops looking into a business like hers was never a good thing.

She looked up as the door opened. "What is it now?" she asked, giving Vasilii a glare.

"We need to know the schedule of the bouncers and door girls for the night Fiana was killed." Vasilii walked into her office, followed by Miroslava, who closed the door behind her.

"What on earth for? No one was on the door when she was killed."

"Because the rifle that killed her was—" Miroslava started to say.

"Never mind why," interrupted Vasilii.

Elena looked at him. She was a woman in her fifties. She didn't smile much because she'd lost three of her teeth in a bar fight when she was in her mid-twenties. She wore the white pancake makeup that was popular in Russia until the arrival of the up-timers, and she was an exceedingly smart and moderately ruthless woman. That's what it took to survive in the world she lived in, and even more to prosper. So she didn't answer Vasilii. He wasn't a cop. If he wanted to cause her problems, he would have to call in favors. And Elena had favors of her own to call in. Even more, Vasilii Lyapunov lacked anything approaching the menace of a *streltzi* cop.

She looked at Miroslava and lifted an eyebrow. That should have been enough, but it wasn't. Then she remembered. Miroslava was an odd one. She no longer owned Miroslava's contract, so Miroslava didn't obey her any more. She looked back to Vasilii. "Why do you want to know?"

"It's part of our investigation," Vasilii said.

"That doesn't answer my question. You already have the man who killed Fiana locked up." She stopped. "You do have the man locked up, don't you?"

Miroslava wasn't good at recognizing other people's expressions, and she was even worse at hiding her own. Elena had known her for years. "You don't have the man who killed Fiana locked up. Is he dead? No. He's not dead, so Feliks didn't do it." She stopped and thought. *If Feliks didn't do it, and they want . . . and Feliks got thrown out the side door, so unless he went around to the front . . .* "Someone got something out of the cloakroom without a ticket!"

Now Elena was furious. Ufa was a very wild town. The safest place to keep anything was on your person. You didn't want to leave anything out where others could get at it. Her cloakroom and the security of the things stored there was vital. If the customers couldn't store their gear safely, then they either wouldn't come to the bar, or would insist on bringing weapons into her club. Either of those meant the end of her business.

"Who else knows?" Elena looked at Vasilii and Miroslava, and seriously considered having them both killed.

"At least two in the city guard," Miroslava said. She wasn't good at reading faces, but she was extremely observant, had a virtually eidetic memory, and was fully aware of just how vital Madam Drozdov felt the security of her cloakroom was, and the lengths she was willing to go to to keep a secret. So she told her that there were others, but not who the others were.

She glanced over at Vasilii, and realized he didn't understand. Vasilii owned her contract and, besides, she liked him. "Madam Drozdov is trying to decide whether it's worth trying to kill us to keep the secret."

"What secret?"

"To keep anyone from finding out that someone got someone else's goods out of the cloakroom."

For a long moment, Vasilii still looked confused. Then he finally got it. "It wouldn't work. Even if she got away with killing us, it wouldn't solve her problem. There are several other people who know, and our deaths would just draw more attention to the issue." He paused and scratched his short beard, then looked at Madam Drozdov. "Your best chance of keeping the fact of the theft quiet is to cooperate with us and hope we can catch the thief. After all, he got into your cloakroom twice. Once while you were open for business, and once after you were closed. Now, who was on duty and when, on the night of Fiana's murder?"

She told them. Like many semi-literate people, Madam Drozdov had a very good, highly-trained memory. She knew the schedule of her employees by heart.

There were three shifts. The night Fiana died, afternoon to evening was Ivana and Alexei, evening to midnight was Kira and Daniil, midnight to closing was Irina and Oleg.

"Good. Thank you," Vasilii said. "When did Feliks arrive at the club?"

Miroslava answered, "Evening shift. The sun was down, so it couldn't be Ivana and Alexei because the rifle didn't arrive until after they were off shift. That just leaves Kira and Daniil and Irina and Oleg."

"We should question them separately."

"Why?" asked Madam Drozdov.

"It's something he read in his books," Miroslava told her with a shrug.

"Because that way they can't adjust what they tell us when they hear what the other person is saying," Vasilii explained. "And you shouldn't be there," he told Madam Drozdov, "because we don't want them too terrified to talk. Do you have a place where we can question them?"

She did.

Kira was nervous when they brought her into the room. She was even more nervous when it turned out that the weird girl was there. But she asked what they wanted.

Miroslava didn't say anything. It was the man. He smiled and asked, "Tell me about the night Fiana was shot."

"I didn't see it. I was looking the other way."

"Not then. Earlier."

"Earlier?"

"Yes. Start when you got to work."

It took a while. They went through her dances. She'd had two sets, then she had server duty, bringing customers drinks and snacks. Then she had door duty, and they wanted to know a lot about that. Who brought in what, did she remember Feliks bringing in his rifle. *Ah,* she thought, *that's what this is about.* She confirmed that she remembered him bring his gun. It was an unusual gun, and he was very proud of it.

"Did he take it out?"

"No, not while I was there."

"Was there any time when you weren't there? During your shift, I mean."

"Well, I had to go to the privy a couple of times."

"Was there any time you were there alone? Did Daniil go to the privy?"

"Yes, but Madam Drozdov doesn't like it when girls are on the door alone, so Daniil got Anatoly to watch the door while he went to the privy. In fact, I remember he sent me to get Anatoly when he had to go."

"Anything odd happen before that?"

"Yes, there was. I remember. There was this man who got soaked with beer when the fight happened. He wanted to know who Feliks and the big guy, Egor, I think, were. Daniil spent a few minutes talking to him."

"What did the man look like, the one Daniil talked to?"

"Kind of average. He was a Cossack, I think. We get some of those. But he wasn't one I remember."

They got hair color, light brown and straight, complexion, brownish tan, beard, a bit scraggly. She didn't notice the eye color, but he didn't seem all that big.

That didn't stop the questions. They went through the rest of her time in the cloakroom before they stopped.

* * *

Even after the interview, Miroslava and Vasilii weren't at all sure what had happened that night. They weren't even one hundred percent sure that Kira wasn't lying to put the blame on Daniil. Not until they called for Daniil and found out that he wasn't in the building. What they were sure of was one of the things that Vasilii knew from his books: witness testimony was not dependable.

"He must have slipped out the side door," Madam Drozdov told them. "Anatoly, you take Oleg and go get him. Bring him back here."

It was about then that Pavel arrived.

"No. Anatoly and Oleg can come along, but Daniil will be coming with me," Pavel said.

* * *

Daniil pulled the wooden case from beneath his bunk and unlocked it. Then he emptied it out onto the bunk while he tried to decide what to take. His room did have a lock on the door, but it was still just one small room.

Daniil was a big man. He topped six feet and two hundred pounds, and from an early age made his way in the world on muscle, not mind. It wasn't that he was stupid. It was more that he'd learned that his strength and willingness to hit people could get him out of the consequences of any mistakes he made. He was simply convinced that he could get away with stuff.

Daniil was gone home when Fiana was shot, and when he got in the next afternoon, the gun was indeed gone, but the ticket was right where it was supposed to be. He breathed a sigh of relief, and tried to forget about the favor.

Then, today, when they took Kira back to ask her questions, he put it together and came to the reluctant conclusion that he wasn't going to be able to get out of this one by knocking out someone's teeth. It was time to leave Ufa, maybe time to leave Czar Mikhail's Russia. The Cossack lands maybe, or General Shein's territory.

Daniil sure wasn't going back to Sheremetev's Russia. He was wanted badly by— He cut off his mental rambling as he examined his third set of clothing. He had three sets, which meant he was moderately well off by the standards of seventeenth-century Russia. He also had a purse that was about half full of paper money and small silver and copper coins. He started putting things in the bag. His second pair of boots. He looked around his small room, then heard something. He went to the door and heard more. He was out of time. He grabbed the purse of coins and the half-full travel bag, went out the door, and down the hallway.

When he opened the backdoor of the small rooming house, he saw two cops on the street. They turned, and Daniil knew he was done, but he wasn't a man to go down gentle. He threw his bag at one of the cops and ran at the other.

As he was running at the man, the cop pulled a polished oak stick out of his belt. It was a new design called a billy club. And Daniil lifted his arm to catch the club and protect his head. It worked, sort of. The club was heavy oak and swung with force. It broke one of the bones in Daniil's forearm, but as much as it hurt, it didn't stop him. He ducked his head and head-butted the cop in the face. Blood was everywhere, and one of the cop's teeth dug into his scalp and they both went down.

Daniil got up, and the cop didn't. But all that took time.

Time Daniil didn't have.

While he was getting up, there was a loud crack, and a sharp pain appeared in his right buttock. His hip was shattered. The ball joint that his thigh bone fit into was no longer attached to the rest of his coccyx. He tried to stand, but any weight on his left leg was agony, and he fell back onto the semi-conscious cop.

Location: Ufa Kremlin, Hospice
Date: April 23, 1637, 7 PM

At the hospice, there was a short battle of authorities. Pavel wanted to question his suspect, and Tami wanted her patient operated on. It took over an hour to get the big man there using a litter, and four men to carry him.

Tami wouldn't be doing the surgery. There were better surgeons than she was in Ufa. Lots of them. Tami was a housewife before the Ring of Fire, and only became a nurse after it. She did study in Grantville, and passed the written test for LPN before she got hired by the czar, and she had copies of just about every up-time medical book in Grantville as of the Ring of Fire. But cutting people open and rebuilding bones wasn't her forte. She was no Sharon Nichols, and she knew it.

Esim, the Tatar doctor, had decades of experience treating sick people, and was used to sewing people up after battles, though before the introduction of sterile instruments and things like iodine and other topical antibiotics, they mostly died of infection anyway.

Her job, as she saw it, was to provide the real doctors with the up-timer information and get out of their way. And, even more importantly, to keep officious cops out of their way.

"We need to question this horse's ass," Pavel Baranov insisted. "There's a murderer out there who's killed two bar girls, and this jerk knows what he looks like. And now the murderer is after the heir to the Chernoff lands."

"Well, why didn't you question him while you were bringing him here? I think he must have lost two pints of blood on the trip. What did you do, ship him by snail?"

"Because every time the men carrying him took a step, he fainted." Pavel tapped the big man's leg and he groaned and fainted. "See?"

"Well, you can stop abusing my patient. You can have him back after he recovers from surgery."

"If he recovers from surgery," put in Esim. "I give him one chance in three, with the amount of blood he's already lost.

And we can't transfuse him without a cross match of his blood. By which time, he may well have bled out. There isn't time to wait. I will have to open him up and sew up the bleeders if he's to have any chance at all. And I have to do it now."

So, in spite of all Pavel could do, Daniil was wheeled into surgery without being questioned.

He never came out.

* * *

Tami wasn't happy with the cops at the moment. Nor, apparently, with Vasilii. "What did you do, Vasilii? I got orders from the czar less than an hour ago that your bar girl attempted murder victim is now a top priority case. I used up the last of the Chlometh on her. I have other patients who need it."

To Miroslava that was good news, if surprising. She'd expected that the baby might get special treatment, but not a bar girl like Marina.

"The father of her child was from an important family," Vasilii said. "And you know the way the world works, even this new world we're building here in Eastern Russia. Even if everyone has equal rights, the rich get their rights paid attention to a lot more than the poor."

"I have wounded soldiers with infected injuries who need that medicine. Men who risked their lives to defend our home."

"And they matter more than a bar girl like me," Miroslava said more than asked. She shrugged. "They always have before. Why should now be any different?"

Tami turned bright red.

Gorg Huff & Paula Goodlett

CHAPTER 6—MOTIVE

Location: Ufa Dacha
Date: April 23, 1637, 9 PM

Miroslava, wearing Vasilii's robe again, and a towel around her hair, walked into Vasilii's room.

"How was your shower?" Vasilii asked.

"Strange, but I liked it. I feel very clean." She looked at him. He was wearing jeans and a shirt, but his boots were off, replaced by slippers. He was sitting at the drafting board with his chair turned to face her. She went across the living room to see what he was doing. The drafting board had a drawing of a boiler taped up near the top and in another place there was a piece of paper with a list of clues. Everything they knew about the Happy Bottom murder and the attempted murder. The rifle, the sight, the crossbow, the witnesses. There was a drawing—well, sort of a drawing—of the alley where Fiana was killed.

She couldn't read the notes, so she asked Vasilii to read them to her. There was a hole in what they knew. A gap, and Miroslava almost had it. Then Vasilii put his arm around her waist and she put it aside for more important things.

Location: Ufa Dacha
Date: April 24, 1637, 8 AM

The next morning, Miroslava woke up knowing what was missing. She went over to Vasilii's drafting table and drew a squiggly line between Marina's name and the word "assassin." Miroslava didn't know how to read or write, so she was making up her own method. The squiggly line translated to something like "unknown connection."

Then she put on her clothes, which were dirty and stank much more now that she was clean, and went to breakfast, leaving Vasilii snoring quietly in bed.

When she got back to the room, Vasilii was sitting in front of his drafting board, wearing his robe, and with his hair wrapped in a towel. He looked up when she came in and asked, "What does the squiggly line mean?"

"How did he know that Marina had a baby? How did he know that it was—"

"Because he asked the clerk, remember."

"Not that. I mean, how did he know that it *mattered*? How did he know that Karol's family cared? Why did he come here in the first place?"

"Those are very good questions," Vasilii said, turning back to the drafting table. "It's possible that he happened to be here for something else." He looked at Miroslava's expression and said, "No, I don't believe it either, but it *is* possible." He turned back to the drafting table. "It would have taken quite a while for him to get here, so someone would have had to send a message sometime ago. It could be a courier, but I sort of doubt it. Even with the war, the radio telegraph system has stayed up and running."

"How does it work?" Miroslava asked.

Vasilii spent half an hour talking about how radios worked, even getting into amplifier tubes and how they worked. He knew the outlines, though not the details, from his time at the Dacha. Miroslava listened, but when he finished she said, "That's not what I meant. How do the telegraph operators get paid?"

Miroslava's face scrunched up in a way that Vasilii was coming to know. He was pretty sure that wasn't exactly what she was after either. Just a step along the path to what she wanted. He remembered an oft-repeated line from his mystery books. "Follow the money." So he figured that finding out how the radio telegraph operators got paid was a step toward finding out what they wanted to know. Whatever that was.

So how do radio telegraph operators get paid? Vasilii didn't know, not in any detail. "I know who we can ask. Well, I think I know who we can ask. The Dacha has a station, and so does the Kremlin. Let's go ask the guys in the Dacha station. It's closer."

* * *

The radio at the Dacha was really three radios. There was the directional set with several antennas that was used for communications, and the broadcast radio that had a range of about fifteen miles and could be picked up by anyone with a crystal set, and the experimental rig where they were trying with no real success to produce FM radio. They were all located in a tower that was four stories tall, and the second tallest building in Ufa. The tallest was the radio tower in the Kremlin. It was six stories tall.

As Vasilii opened the door to the bottom floor of the radio building, he heard music. It was a woman singing in German. She had a furry voice, and there was passion in the song, even if you couldn't understand the words. The music was coming from two speakers across the room. It wasn't loud, at least not so loud that you couldn't talk or think, but it was there.

Between the two speakers was another door. It went through the wall around the Dacha compound and let the public in. There was also a young man, a teenager by his look, sitting at a desk and reading a book. The desk had a sign on it saying "Information." Across from him was a window in the left hand wall with a young woman manning it. Behind the information desk were two doors. Vasilii read the signs over the window and doors. The window sign said "Radio Telegraph Messages." The doors were signed with "Lab" and "Business Office."

"Let's ask the guy at the desk," Vasilii said.

He led the way over, and the teen looked up. "How can I help you?"

"We're trying to find out how telegraph operators get paid."

"That's actually pretty complicated. You need to talk to someone in the business office."

✳ ✳ ✳

Ten minutes later, comfortably seated with fresh, hot, black Russian tea with honey, Vasilii asked his first question. "Why are you being so accommodating?"

Viktor Bogdonovich Fyodorov smiled. "Partly curiosity. Partly we need a new steam engine to get enough juice to expand Dacha radio, and I'm hoping you can move us up in the line a little."

"I'll do what I can, but I can make no promises," Vasilii said. It was a common request. Every time they turned around, there was something else that needed steam power, and needed it desperately. The original Dacha near Moscow was in contact with this Dacha on the quiet. Colonel Leontii Shuvalov knew about the covert messages going each way, but chose to ignore them because they benefitted the old Dacha as much as the Ufa Dacha. So Vasilii knew that the old Dacha was strapped for steam engines too. It wasn't that they weren't making them. It was that there were three needs for every one they made, and new needs popping up way faster than steam engines were.

"Miroslava brought up an interesting question. Since no one person or organization owns all the radio stations, how do the radio operators get paid for transmitting messages?"

Viktor looked at Miroslava with interest, then looked at her with a different sort of interest, one that Vasilii didn't care for at all. "That's a very astute question, Miroslava, and there is a fairly complicated answer. A lot of the network is owned by the government back in Moscow, more is owned by the czar. General Shein owns several. Then there are the independents, individual radio operators who bought or stole their radios and set up in a village somewhere."

"Stole?"

"Sure. More from Sheremetev than from us. He made some examples of radio operators before the czar escaped. A bunch of others took the radios with them when they ran. They found a village somewhere that was within radio range of a couple of other stations, and set up shop."

"Those are the ones I most wonder about," Miroslava said. "How do they get paid?"

Viktor grinned a pleasant grin, and said, "That took some working out. And a fair amount of negotiation, but by now there is a fairly standard rate for radio messages, and it's not that high. Each letter costs three one hundredths of a kopek for each station it goes through. These days almost all the stations have routing books that tell them how many stations and which ones a message will go through to get to the destination.

"For instance, from here to Moscow is twenty-three stations. So it costs point sixty-nine kopeks per letter. Ten letters is six point nine kopeks. Expensive, but less than a courier, unless he's carrying a book. And much faster, especially since all the stations on the ufa to Moscow route have teletypers."

"What's a teletyper?" Miroslava asked.

"It is a machine that works like a typewriter, except it punches holes in a paper tape rather than stamping letters on a sheet of paper. They work both ways. When a message is sent, the signal punches the holes in the tape then you put the tape in a reader, and it only allows contact when a hole in the paper is between the contacts. That way a message can be sent both faster and more consistently with fewer errors. Of course, you have to have the tape, but these days paper tape is manufactured in just about every major town in Russia."

"But how do you pay the operators?"

"They send a listing of how many characters they sent or received from each station every evening, and they get bank credits here or in Moscow, or in some other town, like Nizhny Novgorod. The operators in small towns have to make a trip to a city now and again to pick up the cash. But a lot of the time, it balances out. The telegrapher in such and such a town gets paid by the people in his town who are sending or receiving messages, and uses the credit they get from transmitting other stations' messages to pay for the ones they're sending. It mostly works out. Radio operators keep careful books." He grinned again. "Most of them keep two sets of books. The official books and the unofficial books, since it's illegal to send messages from Moscow to here. From any place in Sheremetev's Russia to here, for that matter."

"So your radio operators would know if someone sent a message from Ufa to the Chernoff family estates?" Miroslava asked.

"If it was sent from this station. But it's as likely that it would go through the royal station in the Kremlin. The fee is the same."

"Would you check to be sure it wasn't from here? We're investigating the murder at the Happy Bottom Club, and we need to know if someone informed the Chernoff family they were about to have a new member."

"Sure. Come with me."

* * *

"Drysi, see if you can help these people out." Viktor shook Vasilii's hand and kissed Miroslava's hand.

"We need you to check your records," Vasilii said as soon as Victor was gone. "We need to know if anyone sent a message to the Chernoff family in the last few months."

"Well, I don't know about months ago without checking my records, but yesterday a Cossack came in and sent a message to the Chernoff townhouse, attention of Karol Ivanovich Chernoff. I noticed because it's not that often we get people in off the street telegraphing Muscovites, especially important Muscovites, and because I had to explain how we charged for messages. He was looking for the cheapest way to get his news across. That's not unusual, but the message certainly was."

"How so?" Vasilii asked.

"It read: Whore dead. Baby alive. Instructions needed. Ufa Dacha. Return Kiril123." Drysi shuddered. "It made me feel kind of creepy, but we're supposed to keep messages private."

"But she's not dead. At least, not yet," Miroslava said.

"No, but he doesn't know that," Vasilii said.

"But wasn't she killed with a rifle? I read about it in the *Ufa Tattler*." The *Tattler* was a newspaper put out by the Ufa Dacha and mostly read by Dacha staff and students, but also available to the rest of Ufa. Many taverns and restaurants in Ufa kept copies, and more than a few hired people to read them to customers. Literacy wasn't common in Russia, but it was in the Ufa Dacha.

"Not Fiana," Miroslava said. "He had to be talking about Marina."

"He probably was," Vasilii agreed, "but that sort of wound is close to universally fatal without surgery and antibiotics." He turned to Drysi and asked, "Has there been a response?"

"Not so far, but it was just sent out yesterday."

"We've got him," Vasilii said.

"Maybe," Miroslava cautioned, but Vasilii could tell she was excited too.

"Drysi, we're going to go check the Kremlin telegraph station to see if there are any messages from earlier. But we do need you to go through your records and see if someone sent a message to the Chernoff family a few months back. And you're probably going to have a cop waiting around here for when this Kiril123 comes back."

"If he comes back," Miroslava said. "What if he sends a runner to pick up the response?"

"Good point. We need a sketch artist."

"What?" Miroslava asked.

"You mean like Mrs. Tupov?" Drysi asked.

Vasilii nodded. Tupov was an artist who spent the better part of her life chafing under the church's restrictions on realism in art. For the last three years, first at the original Dacha, then here, she'd been learning and teaching up-timer art techniques. By now she was quite a good artist. "Send a runner to her, if you would, and ask her if she thinks she could sketch someone just from a description. If she can, I want you to describe the Cossack who sent the telegram to the Chernoff townhouse for her."

Location: Ufa Kremlin
Date: April 24, 1637, 9 AM

The Kremlin telegraph station wasn't manned by talkative teens. It was manned by a sergeant who took privacy very seriously and his duty to the czar even more seriously, which made sense. The Kremlin radio telegraph was used for messages to places like Hidden Valley, where the dirigible base was, and for military intelligence. So they had to get authorization.

That authorization was rapidly forthcoming as soon as they reached someone high enough on the political food chain to understand what was going on.

"It's still going to take a while. There have been a lot of messages to Moscow over the last few months, and a surprisingly large number of them are to important people." He snorted. "Everyone covering their asses."

"In that case we'll be back after lunch. We have some other errands to run."

* * *

Fifteen minutes later, they were in the Morozov tailor shop. Master Morozov was Vasilii's tailor and Vasilii assumed that if Morozov didn't make women's clothing he would know someone who did.

As it happened, Mrs. Morozov made women's clothing. They owned one of the Russian-made sewing machines, and even had pre-made blouses, skirts, and other female attire in various sizes. They would still fit them for the customer, but they had dresses and linen underclothes that would fit well enough for now.

So rather than leaving Miroslava there, Vasilii got to wait while she tried on the dresses to see what fit best and looked best on her.

* * *

After the tailor shop, they went back to the Kremlin and explained what they had learned to Pavel with Colonel Evgeny Aslonav listening in. This was now well up into the realms political.

"Who do you want to send to watch the telegraph, Pavel?" Evgeny asked.

Pavel named a couple of men. "And have them leave their armbands at home." The uniform for the cops was a yellow armband with from one to six black stripes on it, worn over their regular clothing. It was worn over the right sleeve of the tunic and came with a loop that looped over a button on the shoulder. The button itself wasn't much of an indicator of occupation because the brewers had their own armbands. So did tailors, butchers, bakers, and candlestick makers, all of whom wore their armbands when called to defend the walls of Ufa in case of an attack.

Location: Ufa Dacha

The sketch wasn't going well when they got there. First, it was the first time that Mrs. Tupov had ever done anything like this. She worked from people sitting for her or from photographs. Not from "some silly girl who can't make up her mind how big the man's nose is, or how far apart his eyes are."

Second, because every few minutes they got interrupted when said silly girl had to stop to transcribe a radio telegraph message from one of the forms to the teletype tape. That involved her checking the message with the sender, then typing it in—one key at a time, because since you had to punch holes in the paper, each key had to be pressed with considerable force. This keyboard didn't lend itself to touch typing. Hammer typing was more the thing.

Meanwhile, there was nothing for them to do on the case, at least for now. So, they went back to Vasilii's rooms and Vasilii tried to get back to work.

Tried to.

Vasilii didn't work all that well with an insatiably curious young woman leaning over his shoulder, one breast pressed into his back, asking what this part was for, and what that part was for. It was distracting—to put it mildly.

In self defense, Vasilii remembered Bernie's advice to teach Miroslava to read. The Ufa Dacha was well supplied with teachers. So Vasilii hired one.

A HOLMES FOR THE CZAR

✱ ✱ ✱

Svetlana Petrovna was fifteen and had four years of Dacha training. She read and wrote in Russian, Amideutsch and up-timer English. She was good at math. She didn't know what she wanted to be when she grew up, but she thought maybe the first woman to cross the Pacific in an airplane, or maybe a romance writer.

Miroslava found her exceedingly strange. On the other hand, letters made excellent sense. Each sound had a letter and each letter a sound. She could write anything she could say. Or so she thought at first. However, it turned out Miroslava's speech was "peasant" in the extreme.

Russia had less in the way of local accents than other languages. What it had was a clear distinction between "peasant" and "educated" speech. It had to do mostly with enunciation.

Miroslava, in her monomaniacal way, set out to change her accent from peasant to educated. Svetlana Petrovna found herself in the unwilling role of Professor Henry Higgins, stuck with a fanatical Eliza Doolittle.

But Vasilii got to spend the rest of the day working on boilers, condensers, and piping from boilers to engines to condensers and back to boilers. He was trying to figure out a way to get the steam from the boiler in the body of the aircraft

151

to the engines on the wings without losing too much heat. And, so far at least, wasn't having much success.

They didn't receive any messages that day from either the Dacha or the Kremlin. So the next morning, they set out to find out what was going on.

Location: Ufa Kremlin
Date: April 25, 1637, 8 AM

The Dacha telegraph station hadn't found any record of a message to the Chernoff townhouse before the death of Karol Karolivich, so they went to the Kremlin telegraph station, where they were informed rather brusquely that the information had been sent to the city cop headquarters, where it would no doubt be handled by the people whose job it was. With the clear implication that Vasilii and Miroslava should go back to their own affairs and leave guarding the city to those more qualified.

* * *

"Pavel, what's wrong? Did I catch something contagious?" Vasilii asked.

Pavel was at a wooden picnic table stacked high with papers, which were being read by a teenager. Vasilii started wondering if teenagers were taking over the world. "What are you talking about?"

"We were just at the Kremlin telegraph station and were told—not quite in so many words—that we should go back to whatever silly thing we did and leave the policing to the police."

"I'm not surprised. The czar is interested in the attempted murder of Marina. He wants to know if the Chernoff family was involved. It's fairly important because Czar Mikhail sent the news of the new heir to the Chernoff family estates to Karol Ivanovich and he's gotten a message back."

"And what does Karol's papa have to say?" Vasilii asked.

"That they want the baby returned to them for its welfare, and that his aunt, Zia Ivaneva Chernoff, is on her way to Ufa to see to the child's needs."

"Oh, crap," Vasilii said.

"What does that mean?" Miroslava asked.

"It means that Karol's family are running scared, at least a bit," Vasilii said. "No one has seen Director-General Sheremetev in well over a week now, and there are rumors all over the place, everything from Mikhail's uncle having offed him to his having gone to the USE or Spain for allies. Personally, I think it has to be either the Poles or the Turks. Neither one is going to be particularly good for Russia, but one thing I am expecting is that every family that doesn't have a son or a daughter in the czar's service is sending one."

Miroslava was still looking confused.

"The thing is, it's going to be hard for Czar Mikhail to keep Larisa out of her aunt's hands, unless he has solid evidence that the family doesn't have the child's best interests at heart. He can still do it, and probably will, but he will take a hit unless it can be shown that the Chernoff family back in Moscow ordered the child's death."

"So he wants us to catch Kiril123," Miroslava said. "Why won't the cops talk to us?"

"Because they want the credit for catching Kiril123."

"Not me," Pavel said. "My boss and most cops want it to be us that get him. If it were to be learned that a Dacha man and a bar girl caught him while we sat around with, as Bernie would say, our thumbs up our butts, that would make us look really bad. Which is why I am no longer a corporal. I am now a detective corporal and I am in charge of finding Kiril123, not to mention everything else that has gone missing since the czar got to Ufa." He waved at the desk full of papers and the kid.

"I don't care about who gets the credit." Miroslava shrugged.

"Neither do I," Vasilii confirmed. "You be our Inspector Lestrade, and we'll be your Holmes and Watson."

"What does that mean?" Pavel asked.

154

"We solve the crimes, you take the credit," Vasilii said.

"Ha! Miroslava solves the crimes. You just follow her around like a puppy," Pavel said.

"Then I write the casebook about it," Vasilii agreed.

Maksim Borisovich Vinnikov was watching all this with wide eyes. His father was with the *streltzi* contingent that manned the radio telegraph station at the Kremlin, and for the past four years Maksim had been learning reading, writing, and arithmetic. He was, in fact, a fairly avid reader of just about anything, including mysteries. He was also a fair shot, if a bit on the short and scrawny side. His mother wanted him away from anything resembling combat, and she was not fond of the notion of her baby boy out patrolling the wild streets of Ufa. His father, on the other hand—and Maksim himself—wanted him to do something that was at least a little on the martial side.

This was a compromise. Something that would let his papa tell his mama that he was safe in an office, but still had the sort of martial glamour that being a telegraph operator or a lathe operator in the Dacha didn't.

Vasilii Lyapunov hooked a thumb at him. "What about the lad here?"

"A favor. Plus the fact that I can't read more than to sign my name. He will read documents to me and write up the reports. He's learning to be a detective." Pavel looked at him. "What is this? The third lesson or fourth. 'You use what you have.' What we have is Miroslava, who has a strange way of thinking, and Vasilii, who reads a lot. So we use them to get the job done. And we don't need to tell the Colonel about the details of how we do our work."

"Yes, sir."

"What did you learn from the records search at the Kremlin telegraph station?" Vasilii asked.

"Tell them, Maksim."

"Karol Chernoff sent a telegraph to his father the same day he registered the child as his heir. That was December third, 1636."

"What took him so long?" Vasilii asked.

"Who?" Pavel asked.

"The assassin, Kiril123. It doesn't take four months to ride from Moscow to Ufa, not for a single man on a good horse."

"We don't know how long it took him to get to Moscow," Pavel pointed out. "And after that, well, I don't know if you've noticed, but there's been this little civil war going on in Russia and, yes, he can ride around battles, but that takes time too. Especially in winter when you get snowed in at some peasant village for a week if the weather doesn't favor you. I'm not surprised it took him until now."

"You're right. But if he was supposed to kill Marina, there was a good chance, even a probability, that she would still—"

"It was a belly wound," Miroslava said.

"What's the significance?"

"If she'd still been pregnant when she was shot, the arrow would have gone right through the baby."

"But Fiana was shot in the chest," Vasilii argued. "It wasn't just off to the side which is explained by the sight on the rifle. It was high for a belly wound."

"Unless he was unused to long rifles like Feliks' Nadia," Pavel said. "Crossbow bolts drop more over distance than a sniper rifle like that one. A lot more."

Maksim watched the exchange. It wasn't just Vasilii or just Miroslava solving the crime, like Uncle Pavel implied. It was all of them working together, talking it out.

"Do you have people watching the Dacha telegraph station?" Vasilii asked.

"Yes. Nothing yet."

Gorg Huff & Paula Goodlett

CHAPTER 7—MANHUNT

Location: Ufa Dacha Radio Telegraph Station
Date: April 25, 1637, 9:45 AM

Ivan Grigoriyevich Shkuro walked into the telegraph station and saw the cop leaning against the corner. He wasn't wearing an armband, but Ivan knew the look of a cop when he saw one. In fact, it was the lack of armband that alerted him. Most people in Ufa wore some sort of armband all the time now. There was no law requiring it, but after the battle in the field, most wore their armbands as a matter of pride. Strangers to town might not have one, but in general strangers to town didn't have the shoulder button that the armband was attached to.

It was a fairly subtle thing, but Ivan Grigorivich was a careful man, and he noticed such things. Also, he didn't like the way the cop was staring at him.

He almost turned and walked out, but he needed to get the message if there was one. There should be by now. But he was nervous enough so that rather than going to the window, he went to the table and got a sheet of the printed telegraph sheets that you filled out to send a telegraph, and started pretending to fill it out.

He slid a glance at the girl behind the counter. She was trying to be subtle, but not doing a very good job of it. She was directing the cop toward him.

How could they know?

Then he had it. *That bastard! Colonel Chernoff sold me out!*

He turned toward the door and started to leave. A hand came down on his shoulder, and he stooped with the pressure. He used his left hand to pull the knife from his boot, turned, and came up with the knife in his hand. He stabbed the cop in the belly and tried to ram the knife up far enough to reach the heart, but the cop was a big man. His knife didn't make it. It was enough to bring the man down, though. Ivan turned away from the cop on the floor. Then, bloody knife in bloody hand, he ran out the door.

He looked around at the busy street. There were people staring, and he was holding a bloody knife. He threw the knife away and ran.

It was his skill that betrayed him then. His skill and his ignorance, for by reflex, even when throwing the knife away, he tossed it so that the blade went into the muddy ground, leaving the pommel sticking up in the air.

Two blocks away, he found a public fountain and washed his hands and the bloody sleeve. There were other splatters on his clothing, but a bit of blood splatter on your clothing wasn't a rare thing in Ufa, or anywhere else.

* * *

In the telegraph station, there was panic. Lots of panic, and a bit of clear thought. Drysi saw the cop fall and the blood, and then she screamed. But she didn't keep screaming. It was just startlement.

She got herself together quickly. Other people were seeing to the wounded man. Drysi had a phone. It was part of her equipment and it was seldom used. She had it because her other job was going to be a telephone operator, once there was a phone system up in Ufa. Right now there were four phone lines in Ufa, one from here to the Ufa Kremlin radio station, one from the Ufa Kremlin radio station to the czar's office, one from here to Princess Natasha's office, and one from the Ufa Kremlin radio station to the Ufa Kremlin hospice, the only medical center in Ufa. She picked up her phone and plugged the canvas wrapped wire into the socket for the Ufa radio station, and pushed the button that rang the bell there.

It took a moment for them to answer. The phones weren't used much yet. Then, "Hello?"

"Put me through to the hospice. It's an emergency."

"What? What sort of emergency?"

"A cop has been stabbed. We need a doctor now!" she shouted into the phone line.

"Right. Just a second." It was more than a second, but not a lot. more Then the phone rang again, and it rang three times before someone answered.

"Yes? What is it? We're busy here. We don't have—"

"We have a stabbing at the Dacha radio station. We need a doctor as soon as you can get one here."

"Who is this? Is this some sort of joke?"

"No! I'm looking at a cop on the floor of the telegraph office and he's bleeding from a knife wound to his belly."

* * *

From the hospice, word was taken to the cop offices, and more police were dispatched. Along with them came Pavel, Vasilii, Miroslava and Maksim. By the time they got there the doctors already had the man on a stretcher and a pressure bandage over his stomach. They were getting ready to take him away.

A woman who'd been on her way to do the shopping saw the knife thrown. She didn't want to touch a bloody knife, but she did want someone to know about it so she stayed around.

"Hey! There's a knife over here," she told first the stretcher bearers and the doctor that accompanied them. Then she told one of the cops. From there, word went to Pavel.

Pavel looked at Vasilii. "Think there might be those fingerprint thingies you're always talking about?"

"It's worth a look. I remember that you're supposed to wear gloves with that sort of thing, to keep your own fingerprints off it."

"Maksim, you go with Vasilii and get him what he needs. Miroslava, you come with me. I want you in on the interviews with the witnesses."

* * *

Drysi was more helpful this time. The experience of not being able to give a good description the first time made an impression, and she'd tried to take careful note of the salient features. Between that and Miroslava's strange way of looking at the world, they got height and build, also his tunic, pants, coat, and boots. His nose had a bump where it had been broken once. Pavel put out the first official BOLO, Be On the Look Out, in Russian history. There were no radios to send it out on, so it went by word of mouth and runner, to the men who were patrolling the streets, or—more often—having a beer at a tavern in town.

The word of what he was wanted for, one murder and two attempted murders, one of them a cop, had the police force of Ufa, such as it was, actively searching. And, most especially, the guards at the city gates were on high alert. The gates weren't the only way to leave the city. Ufa wasn't walled. The Kremlin was, and the Dacha, but not the city as a whole. There were plans to change that, but they had yet to be implemented.

But there were gates on the main roads into and out of town.

✳ ✳ ✳

Ivan Grigoriyevich was, by then, back in his room at the inn where he'd stayed since his arrival in Ufa. Considering his circumstances, he decided it was better to wait until after dark to leave.

✳ ✳ ✳

Matvey slipped into the common room if the inn. It was one of the better inns on his street, built since Ufa became the capital. And, using quite a lot of the tools and techniques from the original Dacha, it had white painted walls and Coleman lamps for lighting. It had barrels of beer behind the bar, and there was a goat turning on a spit in the kitchen. You could smell it from the common room. The inn also had six rooms to rent upstairs, and a toilet on the second floor.

Matvey knew the bartender and owner pretty well. He ate here about once a week. He didn't pay. That was one of the benefits of being in the city guard.

He went over to the bar and the bartender said, "What will you have?" with a resigned air.

"Just some information. Do you have any Cossacks staying here?"

"A couple. Why?"

"This one is wearing a buff coat over a dirty green linen tunic. His pants are faded red and he wears red boots. He's got light brown straight hair and a busted nose."

"Why do you want him?" the bartender asked.

Matvey didn't reach across the bar and grab the man. He wanted to, but this was too important. All the cops in the city guard knew each other, and aside from being a brown nose, Ilari Karpovich was a good man.

"He knifed a cop! A couple of other people too, but if we don't get him, life is going to get really hard for anyone who helped him." Matvey didn't know how his voice sounded then, but from the way the bartender's face went white, it probably wasn't pleasant. Matvey was happy about that.

"He's upstairs. At least, *a* Cossack of that description is upstairs. But there are a lot of Cossacks in town, what with the possibility they are going to ratify the constitution. And you know how they dress. There could be any number of them with a green shirt and red pants."

Matvey was pretty sure that the bartender was just worried about his place getting torn up, but he did have a point. By now it was common knowledge about Feliks' confessing to a crime that he couldn't have committed while under harsh questioning. Matvey didn't like that, but from his time in the Moscow cops before he came out here, he knew for a fact that Bernie Zeppi had the czar's ear and Bernie didn't approve of torture or cops "abusing their authority." So it was probably a good idea to be careful.

"Okay," he said, using one of the up-timer words that were spreading all over the world for the last five years. "We'll be careful, but I need you to get Efimiia off her lazy bum and have her run to the Kremlin and tell them we might have the guy here."

When the twelve-year-old daughter was brought out, he gave her one of the large copper kopek coins, and told her she'd get another if she got back with the cops in fifteen minutes or less.

* * *

A squad of five cops, including Pavel Borisovich Baranov, arrived in the specified time, and another kopek was passed over. Along with them came Colonel Evgeny Ivanovich Aslonav, Vasilii Lyapunov, and the bar girl Miroslava, who didn't look much like a bar girl any more. She was in new clothes, not wearing the white makeup, and her hair was in a ponytail.

"All right, Matvey," the colonel said. "I reminded the others of this before, but I want this guy alive. He needs to talk before he dies."

* * *

The door had a bar inside. It wasn't a heavy bar, but it was enough to discourage thieves. The room had windows too, but narrow windows—carefully designed so that a man couldn't pass through them—to keep thieves out, but also to keep customers in if they had failed to pay their bill.

Vasilii whispered to Pavel, "Go get the bartender. We need him."

It wasn't long before Pavel was back with the bartender. "We need you to knock on the door and see if you can get him to remove the bar."

"How am I supposed to do that?"

"I don't know. Don't you talk to your customers? Change the sheets, bring them water, something?"

"We change the sheets between customers," the innkeeper claimed, though Vasilii doubted it was true. Having sheets washed was moderately expensive. "And we prefer that the customers use the washroom for washing up. Not that most of them bother to wash up at all."

"Well, think of something!"

"What's this all about?" Colonel Aslonav asked.

"I'm thinking about his crossbow. If we start pounding on that door, he's going to have time to cock it and aim it. If he's standing by the door removing the bar, when we push it open he's not going to have time to do much."

"Not him," Miroslava said. "The girl. The one who fetched us. If she's the one bringing fresh sheets, he's more likely to open for her."

"Go get your daughter!" Colonel Aslonav ordered in a hiss.

"But it's my daughter. She's just a child."

"I will do it," Miroslava said, quietly. And without waiting for a response, she walked over to the door and bent her knees until her head was at the same height as the girl's head if she was standing there. She knocked on the door.

"What?" came from the room.

"Clean sheets, sir," Miroslava said in an excellent imitation of Efimiia's voice.

Sometimes, when Miroslava did things like that, it still shook Vasilii. She'd only heard the girl speak once, for the Lord's sake.

"What's going on out there?" suspiciously in the accent of a Don Cossack.

Miroslava, still with knees bent, gave the cops a harsh look, then said, "You are the third room I've changed the sheets for."

"Come back later."

"But I have to help with the food. I won't be able to change them today if I don't do it now."

"I told you to come back later."

But there were sounds of the man getting up from the bed, then of the bar being moved. Miroslava moved then, pressing herself against the far wall of the hallway as the door started to open.

Matvey slammed his shoulder into the door and bounced. But the door slammed into someone on the other side, and the rest of the squad rushed into the small room, getting in each other's way, and one of them tripping over the Cossack who was on the floor, downed by being hit by the door.

"Keystone cops," Vasilii muttered, but they managed to take the guy into custody without much injury to anyone.

* * *

Ivan Grigoriyevich Shkuro was pretty sure he was a dead man. He was almost phlegmatic about it. The truth was that Ivan had known in his heart that this was how his life was going to end since he was fifteen or so. Well, not this exactly. His best guess was that he'd be killed in a fight. That would have been better, because he was more scared of the torture than the death.

But they weren't torturing him. At least not yet. Instead, he was seated at a table and cloth was folded until it was thick and then dampened with black ink. It was placed before him. He was told to press his finger into it.

"What's this for?" Ivan asked as he pressed his fingers into the cloth as directed. Why not? They could force him if they chose. There were two cops in the room. One a big man with a scar across his face that said he'd survived a sword fight at some point. The other was shorter, with a little star over the stripes on his cop's armband. There was also a woman. She was seated in a chair across from him, and he almost recognized her.

"Fingerprints," said a man in good clothing, as he rolled Ivan's fingers, one at a time, across a sheet of paper. The man had dark brown hair and pale blue eyes in a freckled face. His beard was short, in the modern style that the czar was making popular by example. "I'm Vasilii Lyapunov, by the way."

"What are fingerprints? And why do you want them?"

"These are." Vasilii pointed at the paper, and Ivan could see the lines inked on the sheet. "You left fingerprints on the knife you used to stab the cop in the telegraph office. You also left them on your crossbow, the one you used to shoot Marina. She's still alive. You got that wrong in your message to Karol Ivanovich Chernoff. By the way, how much did he pay you to kill her?"

"Didn't he tell you?"

"He left that part out," Vasilii said with a twist of his lips.

"It figures." Ivan looked at the lines and—not a stupid man—he realized what they meant. He pointed an ink-stained finger at Vasilii's hands. "I take it your fingerprints are different?"

"Yes. Everyone's are. So how much?"

Ivan looked at him and considered. Why not? It wasn't like he owed the colonel anything. "Thirty rubles to kill the woman. She still had the brat in her belly when he sent me and he told me specifically to shoot her there, so I did."

"What about Fiana?"

"Who?"

"The first girl. The one you shot with the rifle."

"How'd you know about that?"

171

"Daniil told us."

"Daniil?"

"The bouncer at the bar. The one you bribed."

Crap! They know everything. "I didn't know her name. That rifle was crap. It didn't shoot straight."

"Why did you use it then?" Vasilii sounded really curious and even kind of friendly.

Ivan shrugged. "Just a stupid mistake. I figured that little jerk owed me something for landing on my table and getting beer and sauce all over me. I figured his rifle was just compensation."

"Why'd you put it back then?"

"After I missed, I knew that if a rifle went missing, it would lead to the bouncer, and from him to me. I figured if I put it back, you couldn't trace it back to me. You'd think it couldn't be that gun, or that the sniper did it. Either way, nothing to lead you to the bouncer or to me."

"It worked," the woman said and he recognized her voice. One of the bar girls but he couldn't remember which. He wondered what a bar girl was doing here.

"This is the strangest questioning I've ever been put to."

The big cop with the scar grunted.

Vasilii hooked a thumb at the big cop. "He's ready to bring out the tongs and the hot coals. But we're after the truth, not a confession."

"We don't need a confession," said the other cop, the one with the star on his armband. "We have plenty of proof you did it."

Ivan decided he didn't much like the cop with the star.

* * *

They continued to question Ivan for about four hours, with breaks, even offering him tea or beer. And by asking the same questions in different orders, mixed with other questions so that it would be hard to keep a lie straight, they got a coherent and probably true account of his dealings with Colonel Karol Ivanovich Chernoff.

The problem was the colonel didn't actually order Ivan to kill the baby, so there was no clear evidence that Colonel Chernoff desired harm to his grandchild. In fact, the colonel never actually said a word about a baby. Ivan had thought he'd be able to get more money from the colonel for killing the kid, after he got to Ufa and learned that Marina had already delivered the child.

With the help of Vasilii, Pavel dictated a report to Maksim, who wrote it out in shorthand, then took the notes back to the Dacha to type up. As yet, the cop headquarters in the Ufa Kremlin didn't have its own typewriter.

What they didn't mention to Ivan was that there was, so far, no response to his message to the colonel asking for instructions.

CHAPTER 8—POLITICS

Location: Czar's Office, Ufa Kremlin
Date: April 26, 1637, 8:35 AM

Mikhail picked up the typewritten report, and began to read. A few seconds later, he turned to his secretary. "I'm going to need to talk to Tami, Bernie, and Vladimir. Also this cop—" He read from the report. "—Pavel Borisovich Baranov. Have them all here sometime this afternoon." Then he went back to reading.

Date: April 26, 1637, 2:45 PM

Pavel wasn't happy. Being called in to talk to the czar wasn't in his job description. It wasn't anywhere near his job description. It was all Vasilii's fault. The other people in the room didn't make him any happier.

At least he wasn't the first one called on.

"How is the child's mother?" Czar Mikhail asked as they were all filing into the Czar's office. He looked at his papers. "Marina, no last name?"

"She is unconscious, and there is a good chance she will stay that way until she dies," Tami Simmons said.

"I ordered that she be given the Chlometh."

"And she was. But it's not a magic wand. You don't just wave it and everything heals. Also, as with all antibiotics, you need a schedule of treatments, and we're short on the drug. So she got what we had, but it wasn't enough for a full course.

"Her small intestine was perforated in three places and the surgeon only caught two of them. Not his fault. It was a small nick, easy to miss, especially if you lack experience. James Nichols probably would have caught it. His daughter Sharon might have. But there isn't a single doctor in Russia who would have caught it."

"Then how do you know about it?"

"Because when her fever spiked yesterday afternoon we went back in and found it. But she's very, very weak, and the infection has gone systemic."

"What you're saying is that we are going to need a guardian for the child," the czar said, looking at Bernie and Vladimir.

"No, that's not what I'm saying. She was conscious for a while and declared her friend Dominika to be the child's guardian in case of her death. She even got the doctor to get one of the clerks in the Dacha to write it all out. And it specifically says that the Chernoff family shouldn't be involved in the raising of little Larisa."

"That's not going to stand, at least not in its entirety, but it might help," Czar Mikhail said.

And Pavel didn't understand. What possible difference could a statement by a bar girl make? It was Karol Karolivich's blood that mattered, not the bar girl's. Then he remembered the clause in the new constitution. "All persons living in Russia shall have equal protection under the law." That was a new thing in Russia, and most people, even most peasants, felt it was just so much flowery language, not something to be taken seriously. This was Russia, not the USE.

At that point, Pavel wished he could have a talk with Vasilii. How could you have slavery and still have equal protection under the law?

Then the czar looked at Pavel. "What about the family? Have they responded to the assassin's telegram?"

"Not yet, Your Majesty. We have people at both telegraph stations, but no messages for Kiril123 have been sent. And Ivan Grigoriyevich Shkuro has confirmed that it wasn't any sort of code. It was just a made up name for him to use in picking up the response."

"Does that happen much?"

"Yes, Your Majesty. For most people, it's easier than an address. Of course, most people use their own name and just add some numbers, so that it's not five hundred messages to Ivan and no way to tell which message is for which Ivan. Vasilii and Miroslava questioned the telegraph operator about that. They even keep a list of used names so that they won't give out a use-name to two customers by mistake."

"Vasilii?"

"Vasilii Lyapunov. He works at the Dacha and has been consulting on this case because of his interest in mystery stories."

The czar looked at Bernie Zeppi.

"He's a pretty good engineer, Your Majesty, and I remember him asking me about forensic science quite a lot. He came to me because he was looking into the murder of a bar girl a few days ago."

The czar looked back to Pavel. "Forensic science?"

"Yes, Your Majesty. Fingerprints and ballistics. Not the kind that measures trajectory. The study of bullets. And a bunch of other stuff, including mug shots and questioning techniques. Questioning techniques that don't include torture. Vasilii's the educated one, but his girl, Miroslava, is the smart one. A real Sherlock Holmes, she is."

Pavel, unlike his boss, was more than happy to give Vasilii and Miroslava credit if it got him out of the czar's presence in one piece.

"Bernie, I want you to have a talk with Vasilii and this Miroslava person, and report back. In the meantime, we need to figure out what to do if the child's mother—" He looked at his notes again. "—Marina, dies. I don't see putting a stripper in charge of Karol Karolivich's bank account."

"Don't let Brandy hear you say that, Your Majesty," Prince Vladimir said with a smile. "Or if you do, let me watch."

The czar gave the prince a look, then he smiled. "Or my wife, nowadays. Those two are as thick as thieves. But I wasn't referring to the young woman's gender. Just her lack of training. And since you're here and clearly so interested in her welfare, you can just take on the role of her financial advisor. Do make sure that she isn't bilked out of Karol's fortune, won't you?"

Prince Vladimir was no longer smiling. But he bowed, and said, "Yes, Your Majesty." What else could he say, given the circumstances?

Location: Hospice, Ufa Kremlin
Date: April 27, 1637, 8 AM

Brandy Bates Gorchakov looked at the two women and the baby, and gave up any notion of condemning Vlad for getting them into this mess. The baby was asleep and snuggled against her mother's side. The mother was red-faced with fever, and the hand that didn't rest on the baby was held by a small redheaded woman who would look better if she wasn't clearly exhausted and cried out.

Yes, Brandy had been a waitress in a bar before and after the Ring of Fire, but she'd never been this sort of bar girl. But she knew that look, and she knew what circumstances could force people to. So, looking at the dying woman, her baby, and her friend, Brandy didn't feel superior or condemning. What she felt was: There, but for the grace of God, go I.

By now, Brandy's Russian was pretty good, even if it did still have a marked West Virginia accent. "Hello, I'm Brandy Bates Gorchakov. How's she doing?"

The redheaded woman tried to stand, caught between obeying protocol and keeping her friend's hand in hers.

"Stay where you are. Sit back down. You don't need to bow to me. Now, how is she?"

Dominika told her. And Brandy got the impression that if she wasn't exhausted and terrified, Dominika's name might well fit her. Brandy could see the girl pouring a drink over someone's head and saying "Take this job and shove it." She liked Dominika already.

Location: Dacha Telegraph Office
Date: April 27, 1637, 8 AM

Drysi was going through the incoming message queue. It was the way they did it. They would send a bunch of messages all together, then switch over to receive and receive a bunch. Then they pulled the tape out and sorted. The teletype reader printed a message, then the next. The tape reader could recognize the code that separated messages, and it rang a bell. Then Drysi pulled the typed sheet out and put in another. That one printed, and repeat. They only printed the messages that were for Ufa. Drysi could recognize the series of holes in the tape that spelled out "Ufa."

The message printed, and Drysi looked at the "to" line. "Kiril123."

She waved the cop over. "Here it is," she said as she read the message.

Fool. We will handle from here. No use for a failure.

No response address was listed. There was a code grouping. A lot of standardized parts of a radio telegraph message had their own simple, short, code group. It shortened the time needed to send. This code grouping meant that no response was required from the recipient.

It came from the Moscow Station as expected. Other than that, there was no sender mentioned.

Drysi typed and sent a request to the Moscow Station asking who had sent it. They probably knew. For that matter, Drysi could make a pretty good guess. But it would help to have confirmation if they would give it.

Four hours later they got a radio telegraph message from one of the Moscow operators. It was indeed from Karol Ivanovich Chernoff.

Location: Vasilii's Rooms, Ufa Dacha
Date: April 27, 1637, 9 AM

Vasilii was at his drafting board and Miroslava was reading a children's book. Well, not exactly a children's book. It was an adult education book, *How to Read*, but it had the standard "see Spot run," as well as pots, pans, fire and other words spelled out with pictures to show what the writing meant. It was one of several such books published by the Dacha back when it was outside Moscow.

There was a knock at the door, and Vasilii went to see who was there. He opened the door. "Bernie? What brings you here?"

"Czar Mikhail's orders," Bernie said. "I'm here to find out what you're doing messing around in the cop's business." Bernie was trying to sound harsh and condemning, but not carrying it off, so he gave up the attempt. "Your murder investigation is bearing some pretty strange fruit. I need you and Miroslava to tell me what you know. According to Pavel Baranov, she's the brains of the outfit."

Vasilii nodded. "She thinks like Sherlock Holmes, or like I think he would think."

"So should she be made a detective in the cops?"

Vasilii looked over at Miroslava, who looked terrified at that idea. "I don't think so. I think that if anything like this comes up again, it would be better to let us be consulting detectives."

Location: Volga River, Steamboat
Date: April 27, 1637, 10 AM

Zia Ivaneva Chernoff looked over at Gleb, her guard and keeper. She didn't cry for her nephew. She hadn't cried for him when he ran off to Ufa, or when he died defending that barbaric outpost. It wasn't that Zia wasn't fond of her nephew. She was sorry for his death. But reality was reality, and family was family. Zia never had any choice in her life. Why should Karol?

Zia was a widow, a recent widow, but not a particularly regretful widow. Her husband was one of the Russian captains lost in the assaults against Kazan last fall. And after his death she was returned to her family, like a load of unneeded cloths. Her brother-in-law would inherit since she'd failed to produce an heir of Grigory's body.

So her brother dispatched her to take care of Karol's bastard daughter, and she suspected that Gleb had different orders in regard to the child if she failed to return it to Moscow. She didn't cry about that either.

The world was what it was.

Two men came out of the river barge cabin. They were younger sons of great houses and were on the boat with the covert approval of their families, though they were both officially disinherited by their families before they ever boarded the barge. Discussions on the trip were of hunting and girls, along with a debate about whether General Boris Timofeyevich Lebedev was good or just lucky. The consensus was lucky until the barge got to Kazan, then it started to shift.

They were here to keep their families from being destroyed should Czar Mikhail win the war. They had no loyalty to much of anything beyond their own position.

Zia sighed. The world was what it was.

Location: Ufa Kremlin, Hospice
Date: April 29, 1637, 3 AM

Marina wasn't breathing. She hadn't been for the last few minutes, and her hand was limp. That too was unchanged. Reluctantly, Dominika let go of the hand.

She didn't know what she was going to do now. According to Prince Vladimir Gorchakov and his wife Brandy Bates, she was in charge of the raising of Marina's baby, and Dominika didn't have a clue what to do. She didn't even know where she and the baby were going to stay.

Location: Ufa Docks
Date: May 1, 1637, 9 AM

Zia Ivaneva Chernoff walked down the gangplank onto the dock. There was no one there to meet her. "Gleb, find us a coach. I have no intention of walking on muddy streets in these shoes."

Gleb gave her a look, but went to fetch a coach. What he came back with half an hour later was a wagon pulled by what looked to be a plow horse.

"What's that?"

"All I could find." Gleb didn't seem any happier with the situation than she was.

✳ ✳ ✳

A few minutes later, dismounting the wagon at the gates of the Ufa Kremlin, her feet landed in a large puddle of muddy water. "Are we being shown our place in the world, do you think?" she asked Gleb.

Gleb didn't answer. He didn't even shrug.

＊ ＊ ＊

"Sorry no one was at the docks to meet you," Vladimir Gorchakov said when he entered the sitting room where Zia was waiting impatiently. "We were at a funeral."

"Anyone I should care about?"

"Marina, the mother of your grand niece," said a woman who Zia assumed must be Brandy Bates.

"Well, that simplifies matters, though it will require that I obtain a wet nurse for the babe," Zia said. "Who do I see about a river boat to take us back? I have no desire to stay in this—" She sniffed. "—place any longer than necessary."

The truth was that Zia was frightened. The up-timers were powers, delivered to this century by the Lord God for reasons only he knew. She knew perfectly well that Bernie Zeppi was revered in Moscow as almost a saint after what he did about the slow plague that struck Moscow in the spring. And she knew that it was worse this year than any time since Bernie arrived in Russia, though not as bad as it had been before.

All that meant she was dealing with people of power, a kind of power that she didn't understand. It made her afraid, and that made her belligerent.

"Not so fast," Prince Vladimir said. "Marina named a guardian for her daughter before she died."

"Who? You?"

"No. A woman named Dominika, though Czar Mikhail has asked us to give Dominika any assistance she needs in dealing with her new charge."

"Dominika who?"

"Just Dominika." Brandy said. "A long time friend of Marina."

"Another whore?" Zia blurted, almost shrieked. "A whore taking care of my grand niece?"

"Well, a bar girl, in any event," Brandy Bates said with a wide smile.

"The family will never stand for this."

"Where is Sheremetev?" Vladimir asked, and there was no smile on his face at all. "Your side, your family's side, is missing its leader. As of this moment, all the wealth, all the lands of the Chernoff family, whether here or back in Western Russia, is the property of Larisa Karolevna Chernoff, and it's under the care of Dominika. Your brother backed the wrong horse."

"You haven't won yet!"

"No, not yet. But that's why you're here, because your brother is very much afraid that we will win."

"I am here to see to the welfare of a member of my family," Zia lied through her teeth. "Even if she is illegitimate."

Location: Vasilii's Rooms, Ufa Dacha
Date: May 1, 1637, 12:15 PM

There was a knock at the door and Miroslava went to see who it was. It was Dominika, dressed in conservative clothing, with puffy eyes, but a firm expression.

Miroslava opened the door farther, and Dominika said, "You weren't at the funeral."

Miroslava blinked. It was true. She knew that Marina was being buried next to Karol today, but Miroslava didn't like funerals, and didn't really understand the need for them. Besides, Vasilii needed to work on the airplane steam engine and Miroslava had reading and writing lessons. She didn't know what to say, so all she said was "No, I wasn't."

"Everyone was there. Madam Drozdov closed the club and all the girls and the bouncers came."

That was a surprise. Madam Drozdov didn't give up income for anything except the chance of more income. "What did she want from you?"

"What everyone wants. Karol's money that is Larisa's money now. She offered to let me out of my contract if I were to invest in the club. She wants to send to Moscow for more girls." She looked at Vasilii. "Why did the czar give all that money to Larisa?"

"Come in, Dominika," Vasilii said. "Have a seat, and we'll talk about it."

It turned out, over the next half an hour or so, that Dominika didn't trust anyone to give her unbiased advice. Yes, Vladimir and Brandy seemed nice, but someone like them being nice to someone like her . . . well, they just had to be after something. Madam Drozdov was suddenly nice, and that was even more suspicious. All the girls were nice, and that might be all right, except most of them had asked her for money at the funeral. And she figured the ones who hadn't were just a little more subtle.

"Then why come here?" Vasilii asked. "If you can't trust anyone, why trust us?"

"You didn't come to the funeral. Miroslava is weird. She always has been. But she never tried to do me out of a tip, or steal one of my customers. And, well, she has you. And she's smart. All the girls knew that. Weird, but smart."

"That's actually quite well reasoned," Vasilii said, sounding surprised. Which got him a glare from Dominika and a head shake from Miroslava.

"You can probably trust Vladimir and Brandy. At least what they tell you will probably be true. They do have an ulterior motive, but it's not aimed against you. It's mostly aimed in favor of Larisa because Czar Mikhail wants the child to stay here in Ufa, at least until the war is over. And after the war is over, he wants the lands and property of the Chernoff family in the hands of someone loyal to the crown. Which Karol Ivanovich Chernoff is not."

"They aren't going to let me keep Larisa," Dominika said.

"Maybe not," Vasilii agreed. "I'd guess that the Chernoff family will challenge everything they can think of in the courts. Karol's legitimizing of the baby, Marina's rights to the baby if it is legitimate, and Marina's making you her guardian.

"They will lose the first. Czar Mikhail has already made that clear. But they may not necessarily lose the other two. If I were you, I would look for a compromise."

"What sort of a compromise?"

"I don't know," Vasilii said.

"You keep the child, and enough money to let you raise her as a noble, and they keep the rest," Miroslava suggested.

"The Chernoff family might go along with that, but I doubt that the czar would."

"Why not?" Dominika asked.

"Because he wants the money, that wealth, all those resources and serfs in the hands of someone loyal to him, not to Director-General Sheremetev."

"But they aren't. They are back in Moscow and in Western Russia. Larisa isn't really in charge of any of it."

"I'm not a general, but as of right now, today, Czar Mikhail is winning the war. That could change, but the momentum is shifting in Czar Mikhail's direction. So if those lands aren't in Larisa's little baby hands right now, they likely will be sooner or later. This is just my opinion, but what I think the czar is worried about is the next war—or, rather, avoiding the next war."

"So how does giving the Chernoff money to Larisa help with that?"

"If it's being used for jewel-encrusted bassinets, it can't be used to hire an army. Or, more accurately, to contribute to hiring an army. And Czar Mikhail is assuming that you, as Larisa's guardian, will be more loyal to him than Karol Ivanovich Chernoff is."

Dominika was not a stupid woman. She was no towering genius, and she was very lacking in education, but if a problem could be explained in a way she could understand, she could mostly grope her way to a solution.

There were also a lot of things that Dominika was aware of simply because everyone in Russia who wasn't totally brain dead was aware of them. One of those things was that the very same day that the czar ended serfdom, the Gorchakov family, in the person of Natasha Gorchakov, had forgiven the debts of all the serfs in her lands. And Dominika also knew perfectly well how to take a strong bargaining position so that she could be talked down to the price she wanted. So, gradually, she started to smile.

"How would I go about letting the Chernoff family know that I am considering making a proclamation that all the serfs on all Chernoff lands have their debts forgiven? I haven't done it yet, but I, as Larisa's guardian, am considering it."

Location: Small Conference Room, Ufa Kremlin
Date: May 2, 1637, 12:15 PM

Not all that long ago, the Kazak Khan Salquam-Jangir sat in that very chair, Vladimir thought as Zia Ivaneva Chernoff sat down. Across the room, Dominika sat in the chair that Czar Mikhail had used. In another chair, the wetnurse held baby Larisa Karolevna Chernoff, and next to Dominika sat Brandy. On her other side, sat Vasilii's girlfriend Miroslava.

Vasilii was seated next to Miroslava, and Vlad went to sit next to Brandy. Zia Chernoff was outnumbered by rather a lot, but then, she didn't have an army investing the city.

"Turn the child over to me now, girl," she said to Dominika, "or it will go very badly for you." There was, in her tone, an automatic assumption of authority, as though she were speaking to a slave in her household. A slave who was suspected of theft.

For a moment, Dominika cringed back in her seat, and Vlad was getting ready to intervene. Then Miroslava passed a sheet of paper over to Dominika. "If they are going to be that unreasonable, perhaps you should go ahead and forgive the serfs' debts now."

Dominika picked up the sheet, and examined it, though Vlad knew that she couldn't read very well.

"What is that?" Zia Chernoff asked.

Miroslava looked at Dominika, who shrugged. So Miroslava handed another sheet to Vasilii, who leaned over to hand it to Zia Chernoff.

As it turned out, Zia wasn't a reader. She was having as much trouble reading the short text on the sheet as Dominika would if she didn't already know what was there.

I, Dominika, for my Charge, Larisa Karolevna Chernoff, in accord with my understanding of both her mother's and her father's wishes, do hereby forgive all debts owed by all serfs in all the lands owned or held by the Chernoff family. Any and all slaves held by any member

of the Chernoff family anywhere in the world are, as of this moment, manumitted by the hand of Larisa Chernoff.
I do this in support of Czar Mikhail's proclamation of liberty for all the serfs, and to encourage all the serfs and slaves in the Chernoff lands in their loyalty to the czar.

"You would ruin us all, even Karol's bastard daughter," Zia said, shocked.

"Not entirely," Vladimir said. "The lands themselves are worth quite a lot, and with the new plows and other technology, you don't need nearly as many serfs to till a plot of land. Not that the Chernoff family won't take a hit. We did, after all. But just think of how much it will lighten the load on your souls when you come before your maker."

"You can't. We won't allow it." But, somehow, that tone that expected automatic obedience, was missing now. Zia, in spite of the words, was begging now, not commanding.

"I haven't," Dominika said. "At least, not yet. But you can't prevent me should I decide to."

"What do you want?"

"I want what Marina wanted, and what your nephew wanted. I want what's best for Larisa. I want her to be able to grow up strong, healthy, and free, with all the tools and skills she will need to make her way in the world as she wants to. I don't want her sold to a brothel keeper or to a husband. I want her to have her own name, held in honor and free of taint."

✱ ✱ ✱

The truth was more complicated and less pure than Dominika was painting it here. She did want all those things for the baby. She wanted them because she was pretty sure that was what Marina would have wanted. But that wasn't all Dominika wanted. She also wanted to live well in her own person, to have a name, and nice dresses, and servants, and all those other things that she imagined the wealthy to have.

But she was smart enough to realize that her best route to all those things was to cleave as closely as she possibly could to Marina's baby girl.

✱ ✱ ✱

Zia looked at the whore across the table and was impressed in spite of herself. She wished that there had been someone who cared about her the way Dominika claimed to care about Larisa. She, after all, had been sold to a husband to benefit the family. It hadn't been a pleasant marriage. Her husband had despised her almost as much as she had despised him. The fat fool called her an ugly cow on their wedding night, and their relationship had gone downhill from there until his death in the battle of Kazak. General Tim had done her a favor, even if the fat fool's family had sent her home in disgrace.

"You know, a new world is coming," Brandy Bates told her. "You can be a part of it. You don't have to go back to Moscow. You can stay here."

✱ ✱ ✱

Dominika turned to Brandy Bates in shock. This wasn't something she had considered, and it wasn't something that she was happy about either. First, because Dominika wasn't at all sure how long she could keep up a front with these nobles, but it darn sure couldn't be long. She was a bar girl, not a noble. She had no idea how to act like a noble, not for more than an hour's entertainment, not for real. And as soon as they discovered who she really was, she'd be back in the bar, and Larisa wouldn't live to be grown.

Second, because she didn't trust this woman. This woman who was going to take advantage of her because she could, because she was the real noble. It might be different if it were Brandy or Natasha. They had more reason to help her than to hurt her.

But Zia Chernoff was the sort of noble who leaned off their horse or out of their carriage, and spat on the likes of Dominika.

Dominika didn't know what to say.

She looked at Zia Chernoff, a flat-faced woman with graying hair, in white pancake makeup, with black eyes and overweight. "Not in my house!"

That was bragging. Dominika didn't have a house. She had a room in a boarding house, and not a good one. For the past few nights she'd been sleeping in the hospice ward where Marina died and where the wet nurse for the baby worked as an aide.

She saw Zia Chernoff's face go hard and didn't care. She felt her own face go hard and stubborn.

"As if I would stay with the like of you. If the baby and I stay here, you won't be—"

"The baby," Brandy Bates interrupted, "will be staying in Ufa for the foreseeable future and in the care of Dominika, as was the final wish of her mother."

"And what of her father?"

"Her father made no declaration, save to recognize the child. There is nothing in anything he wrote to indicate that he would object to Dominika."

"Karol liked me!" Dominika said, and it was true. She had often been Marina's guest and Karol would take them both out for dinner or to a puppet show.

"Karol was a boy, his head turned by a pretty face."

"Karol Karolivich Chernoff was the only member of the Chernoff family to show loyalty to the czar," Vladimir said coldly. "His will, as expressed in his formal recognition of the child, and Marina's in her dying declaration, are what rules here. Larisa Karolevna Chernoff is the heir to the Chernoff lands, and her primary guardian is Dominika. That has been decided!"

The face under the white pancake makeup was, Dominika thought, white with shock. Dominika started to smile.

Then Brandy Bates started talking. "Everyone settle down." She turned to Dominika. "Listen to me, woman. You need her. I know. I worked in a bar myself. I was just serving beers, not dancing, but I know how different the world is. You will need her help in navigating the intricacies of Russian court life." Then she turned to Zia. "And you need her. Not just because she has the authority here, not you, but because there are parts of this new world that she knows better than you do. Both of you need to pull in your horns a little and try to come up with a compromise that will work."

Finally, for the first time, Dominika and Zia found something in common, as they both looked at Brandy Bates and wondered what in the world "pull in your horns" meant.

It broke the tension.

Gorg Huff & Paula Goodlett

EPILOG

Location: Stefan Ruzukov's Gun Shop
Date: May 3, 1637, 8:15 AM

Stefan waved Egor Petrovich to a chair. "I have some news for you."

"Is Feliks going to hang?" Egor asked hopefully.

"Feliks didn't do it. It was a paid assassin from Moscow."

"That makes no—" Egor started hotly.

Stefan interrupted. "Yes, it does, if you know the whole story." Stefan then told him the story as he'd gotten it from Vasilii and Miroslava.

Egor didn't like it. He wanted to believe that it was Feliks. He didn't want her to have died by chance because the shooter missed his real target. It was unfair, but both of them knew perfectly well that the world was unfair.

"What about the baby?" Egor finally asked.

"The baby is the head of the Chernoff clan." Stefan smiled. "And I imagine that Karol Ivanovich Chernoff is pretty unhappy about that."

"What about him? I know he's back in Moscow, but when the czar wins?"

"No proof that he wanted the child dead."

"So what? He ordered Marina murdered. 'Equal protection under the law.' That's what the new constitution says."

"Yes, it does, but those laws don't stretch back to before they were written. For him to have murdered Marina under the old law was cause for a fine, and that's all."

"That's not fair!"

"I agree." Stefan shrugged his disappointment.

Location: Czar's Office, Ufa Kremlin
Date: May 3, 1637, 11:45 AM

Czar Mikhail got up as the door opened and moved around his desk to the table in another part of the large room. He waved his guests to the table. They went to it, but no one sat until he did.

His guests were his wife, Vlad and Brandy, Bernie and Natasha, and Olga Petrovichna. There were a number of things on the agenda, and once everyone was seated, Mikhail rang a small silver bell and another door opened. A table on wheels was rolled in, and three palace servants served them lunch, then left.

Spreading mayonnaise on a slice of bread, Mikhail asked, "What's first?"

They went through the new nobles that had arrived in the last week. It was a mixed bag, mostly great families trying to cover their asses. And that led them to Zia Chernoff and the situation with Karol's daughter.

"I think I have convinced them to move in together," Brandy said. "Larisa needs to learn the etiquette of court, if you're serious about making her the head of the Chernoff family?" Brandy's voice rose in question.

"Karol Ivanovich Chernoff is going to find himself with a bald spot and living in a monastery," Czar Mikhail said, "if he doesn't find himself in a hole in the ground. I don't like people who order the murder of children, and that goes double for those who order the deaths of their own grandchildren. Besides, Karol was a good kid. He deserved better from his family."

"In that case, it's important that we get Zia on our side," Vlad said. "Because even if Dominika is the one in authority, there is no way she can negotiate the politics."

"Do you think there is any real chance of that?" Czarina Evdokia asked. "I remember Zia as a sour-faced woman who didn't like anyone."

"We need to try, Your Majesty," Vlad said.

"Okay. Talk to my secretary. We will arrange to have them visit the palace occasionally and let the children play with the baby. Both to let Dominika get used to court life and to let Zia Chernoff know that we mean it about Larisa being noble."

Brandy made a note on a tablet next to her dinner plate. She hadn't touched her sandwich yet.

"Remember," Bernie said around a mouth full of sandwich, "if it weren't for Vasilii we never would have found out about the baby, at least not before it was dead."

"Not Vasilii. He's just Miroslava's Doctor Watson," Brandy said, then added, "You sexist pig."

Bernie held up his hands in innocence. "What'd I do?"

"Yes, we probably ought to do something for Miroslava," Czar Mikhail agreed. "Where is she from? At the least, we can give her a last name."

"I don't know," Vlad said. And as he looked around the table, there were only shaking heads.

Bernie grinned. "Well, in that case, I recommend that her name should become Miroslava Holmes."

"Good enough. And while we're on this subject, Olga, I want you to have someone look at those contracts those girls at the Happy Bottom have. See what you can do about making them a bit less one-sided."

Location: Hotel Room, Ufa
Date: May 10, 1637, 9:35 AM

Detective Sergeant Pavel Baranov looked down at the body on the expensive Indian rug. There was a hole in the man's chest and blood had soaked the rug. No one had heard a thing last night, and the door was locked from the inside, or had been, before his men busted it open.

He looked over at Maksim. "Run to the Dacha, lad, and tell them I need Miroslava Holmes."

Gorg Huff & Paula Goodlett

AUTHOR'S NOTES

It's said that the north has two seasons: winter and construction. Czar Mikhail and his party arrived in the middle of construction. But this was not 1631, with one little center of the computer age in a wide world of early modern.

This was 1636, by which time Russia was tied together by hundreds of short range (five to ten miles) crystal radio transmitter/receivers. A Russia where there were hundreds of businesses based on up-time designs spread all over western Russia. Road builders and book makers, printer and paper makers, tailors and shoemakers, batch production cement makers, foundries and copper wire makers. Steam barges were taking fish caught in the Caspian Sea and shipping them all the way up to Moscow, and returning to the Caspian with loads of cloth, pots and pans.

That's a lot of people working in new trades all over Russia, and while not all of those workers were happy about the way they were being treated, very few of them blamed the czar, or even the Dacha. Part of that was because the primary sources of news from the rest of Russia (the radio telegraph operators) were in favor of the Dacha and the czar. Most of them were trained at the Dacha, after all.

When the czar made his Emancipation Proclamation, he got a lot of takers, and not just among the peasants. It wasn't half the people in Russia. It wasn't even a tenth part. However, it was plenty to turn the outpost of Ufa with its population of less than a thousand into one of the larger cities in Russia in the space of a few months. Between July and November of 1636, Ufa went from a population of less than a thousand to a population of more than twenty thousand, if you include the outlying villages

The steamboats on the Volga meant that a lot of those people were able to bring their gear with them. That gear along with the workforce and a bit of city planning unhindered by prior ownership and encouraged by the knowledge that *"winter is coming"* (cue ominous music) produced a ***lot*** of construction in a relatively short time.

* * *

That construction was barely touched on in *1637: The Volga Rules* and only a bit more in *The Happy Bottom Murders*. But it's important to remember that while the great and mighty are deciding the fate of the world, and while plots are unfolding and being exposed, most people are busy trying to put food on the table and make sure they have a roof, walls, and enough firewood when the snow starts to fall.

And they will go right on doing that, whether it's convenient or inconvenient for kings and potentates, or even authors.

And finally: Even more than the people of the Gorchakov Dacha outside Moscow, the immigrants to Ufa are self-selected go-getters. The ticket punchers stayed in Moscow, or whatever town or village they lived in.

CHARACTER LIST:

Alexei: Bar guard

Anatoly: Bouncer at The Happy Bottom

Aslonav, Evgeny Ivanovich: Cop commander *dvoriane* minor service nobility.

Baranov, Pavel Borisovich: Cop who becomes the first Detective in Ufa

Buturlin, Timofei Fedorovich: Colonel, Garrison Commander, Ufa

Chernoff, Karol Ivanovich: Karol Karolivich's father

Chernoff, Karol Karolivich: well to do soldier, killed in battle, leaves Marina behind

Chernoff, Larisa Karolevna: Karol's daughter by Marina

Chernoff, Zia Ivaneva: Karol Chernoff's aunt, sent to Ufa

Daniil: Bar guard

Dariya: Bar girl

Dominika: Bar girl, Marina's special friend

Drozdov, Elena: Owner of The Happy Bottom. Insists on being called Madam.

Drysi: Telegraph operator

Egor Petrovich: Employee of the gun shop

Esim: Tatar doctor

Feliks Pavlovich: Sniper, murder suspect.

Fiana : bar girl

Fyodorov, Viktor Bogdonovich: Radio manager at Dacha station

Gorchakov, Brandy: Up-timer, counselor to the royal family

Gorchakov, Vladimir Petrovich: Boyar, Counselor to Czar Mikhail

Holmes, Miroslava: Our Sherlock Holmes, starts out as a bar girl. She has hazel eyes and auburn hair, she is five seven.

Ilari Karpovich: stabbed cop

Irina : bar girl

Ivana : bar girl

Kira: bar girl

Kotermak, Yuriy: Ufa city Garrison Sergeant.

Lyapunov, Vasilii: Engineer geek, Ufa Dacha

Marina: Bar girl. Karol's lover and mother of Larisa

Matvey: A beat cop

Nadia: Feliks' rifle

Oleg: Bar guard

Olga Petrovichna: effectively the mayor of Ufa

Roksana: Bar girl

Ruzukov, Stefan Andreevich: Factory owner in Ufa and recently advanced to *dvoriane*

Ruzukov, Vera Sergeevna: Delegate to Constitutional Convention, called "The Honorable."

Shkuro, Ivan Grigoriyevich: Cossack known to Karol Ivanovich Chernoff

Shuvalov, Leontii: - Colonel in Russian Army for Sheremetev in charge of the Gorchakov Dacha

Simmons, Tami: Nurse and Surgeon General for Mikhail's Russia

Vinnikov, Maksim Borisovich: Teenage reader and detective in training for Pavel Baranov

Waldemar: mortuary attendant

Made in the USA
Columbia, SC
27 November 2020

25633076R10117